In the Clear

ANNE LAUREL CARTER

ORCA BOOK PUBLISHERS

Canadian Cataloguing in Publication Data
Carter, Anne, 1953–
In the clear

ISBN 1-55143-192-0

I. Title.
PS8555.A7727I65 2001   jC813'.54   C2001-910131-7
PZ7.C2427In 2001

First published in the United States, 2001

Library of Congress Catalog Card Number: 2001086678

Orca Book Publishers gratefully acknowledges the support for our publishing programs provided by the following agencies: The Government of Canada through the Book Publishing Industry Development Program (BPIDP), The Canada Council for the Arts, and the British Columbia Arts Council.

Cover illustration by Ron Lightburn
Cover design by Christine Toller
Printed and bound in Canada

IN CANADA:
Orca Book Publishers
PO Box 5626, Station B
Victoria, BC Canada
V8R 6S4

IN THE UNITED STATES:
Orca Book Publishers
PO Box 468
Custer, WA USA
98240-0468

03 02 01 • 5 4 3 2 1

The author would like to acknowledge the support of the Canada Council and the Ontario Arts Council.

For Janet Abernathy

and

Mary Richardson,

who gave me their stories.

1.
FACE-OFF, 1959

"It's *Hockey Night in Canada*," I holler. My voice swells in a perfect imitation of my favorite TV announcer, Foster Hewitt, on a Saturday night.

"In goal for the Montréal Canadiens ... Jacques Plante."

"Quiet, Pauline!" my mother scolds from the kitchen. "I'm on the phone. Long distance to Grand-mère in Montréal."

"In goal for the Maple Leafs ..." I raise my voice a notch louder. Grand-mère is a Canadiens fan. "... Johnny Bower!" Time for a whistle, long and shrill. Grand-mère knows that the only thing I enjoy more than hockey is making my mother good and mad.

High heels click across the kitchen floor.

I wait. I push my thin, shrunken left leg to one

side of my throne, the cushioned window seat over-looking our backyard. I used to wait for my mother's home-school lessons at the kitchen window at the front of the house. I used to watch for my old friend – my old best friend – Henry Patterson, walking to school with Stuart O'Connor and Billy Talon. Until one day a new girl on our street stopped and pointed at me. "Look!" she yelled. "Is that Polio-Pauline? I heard she caught it from the Don Mills pool." Four girls turned and stared at me. I stuck out my tongue and they ran, afraid they might catch it.

On my window seat, I position the little metal men on my dad's old table-hockey game for a face-off. My dad and I are big Leafs fans. We're hoping we'll win the Stanley Cup this year. When I play hockey on the window seat at the back of my house, the blue paint-chipped Maple Leafs never lose.

"Pauline!" My mother stares from me to the hockey game to the stack of books she left within reach this morning.

I never reach for the books she leaves me.

Her voice accuses me of betrayal. "You haven't read a thing all morning!" She grabs my table-hockey game and turns away. The accordion pleats of her gray flannel skirt flick the air. Before I can stop her, she's locked my game in a cabinet on the other side of the room.

"No fair," I yell. My metal leg brace is off and my crutches are on the floor.

"You refuse to read the books I give you! You do it to annoy me."

Now I turn away. Outside the window, I see my dad skating figure eights around our new backyard rink. He flies by, waving to me. He's so pleased with himself for finally building a rink this winter. My mother wasn't keen on the idea. Every year she gave more reasons. Like, what if there's a thaw and water floods the basement? What if a puck breaks a window? Who's Dad going to play with? What if kids sneak over the fence in the middle of the night and get hurt? My mother can be such a dream squelcher. But this year – maybe it's the Stanley Cup fever – Dad ignored her and built it anyway. Our wide backyard is meant for a rink, he says. The wooden fence on both sides makes natural endboards when he shoots pucks. He bought nets and froze them into the ice. Years ago, he played hockey at high school and university, and now when he goes out to skate, he's dreaming he plays for the Leafs.

If only I could fly out there with him, so powerful and free.

Suddenly I see Henry, my once-upon-a-time best friend. He's jumping over the fence, the endboards, wearing his skates. He begins to race around the rink with my dad. Henry plays on a Don Mills hockey team – I've watched him leave for a hundred games with that big, black bag of his. He's fast, almost as fast as my dad.

What a show-off! Wouldn't you know he'd be the first kid out with *my* dad on *my* new rink?

I thump the window. Henry looks up. I glare, stick out my thumb and jerk it sideways, the unmistakable sign for *go away*, my gesture to Henry from the time I was in the hospital and did not speak for months.

"This could be Grand-mère's last Christmas," my mother says, her voice soft with apology and regret. She never stays mad at me for long.

Henry's shoulders droop. My dad says something before he leaves. Dad likes Henry. If the Leafs make it to the playoffs, he'll ask Mr. Patterson and Henry to watch a Saturday night game with us. I'll hate it. Dad thinks I'm alone too much, but it's way better, just Dad and me. If Henry comes, I'll hide my leg under a blanket and I won't cheer or say a word. I still don't speak when Henry's around.

I turn to glare at my mother. Her hands fuss nervously with the perfect bun at the back of her head. "She wants to come visit us, but she can't travel alone."

"Can't someone bring her?"

"No. My sisters are busy with their families. All your cousins want to stay home for Christmas."

We usually celebrate Christmas at Tante Giselle's or Tante Mireille's in Montréal. My parents think it's good for me to see my cousins. But last year we drove through a blizzard and my mother swore, "No more winter driving. What would happen to Pauline in an accident, or, God forbid, if something happened to all of us?"

My cousins hate me. They play games with balls and I can't chase the ball. I complain to my mother and she makes them get it for me. Behind her back, my cousins call me "Tattle-tale." I hate them every bit as much as they hate me.

But I have another aunt. She's the black sheep of the family and I adore her.

"Tante Marie isn't married," I say. "You could ask Tante Marie."

"You know how hard I find her visits. She interferes. She likes to stir up trouble." My mother's nervous hands smooth her perfectly ironed skirt.

Tante Marie is my mother's youngest sister, ten years younger. Where my mother is hard bones and smells like a closed-up library, Tante Marie is soft skin and smells of lavender and the open woods. Her dark hair is never pinned back but curves playfully around her shoulders. She makes my father and me laugh and she's not afraid of anything or anybody.

Something always happens when she visits – some wonderful trouble.

There are only two weeks until Christmas.

My mother reaches for the top book. "*The Secret Garden.* You'd like it. There's a girl in this book almost as old as you and a boy in a wheelchair."

She flips open to the first page.

I reach for my crutches, ignoring my brace. It takes too long to fasten around my left leg and I want to make a fast getaway. "I don't want to hear about a cripple."

She starts to read, "When Mary Lennox was sent to Misselthwaite Manor to live with her uncle everybody said she was the most disagreeable-looking child ever seen ..."

Without my brace, I lean heavily on my crutches to hurry out of the back room, into the front hallway. On my left is the kitchen. My mother's domain. On my right, stairs lead up to my parents' bedroom and the guestroom. I can't do stairs easily. My bedroom is here on the main floor, close to the side door. But my bedroom doesn't have a lock on it.

In front of me is the bathroom. It's my only choice. I lock the door behind me.

Her voice is slightly muffled. Too bad. I can still make out every word.

"So when she was a sickly, fretful, ugly little baby she was kept out of the way, and when she became a sickly, fretful, toddling thing she was kept out of the way also."

I flush the toilet, over and over. For a while, all I can hear is the sound of water rushing through pipes behind walls and under the floor.

I stop. The last drips of water fill the toilet tank.

"There was panic on every side, and dying people in all the bungalows. During the confusion and bewilderment of the second day Mary hid herself in the nursery and was forgotten by everyone."

I open the door a crack and thrust out my hand. "Okay. You win. I'll read it. But on one condition. You invite Tante Marie."

There is the sound of a book being slammed shut. Pages pressing, words colliding. Trouble.

I feel the strong spine of the book placed between my thumb and fingers.

"Okay," she says. "*You* win. I'll invite Tante Marie."

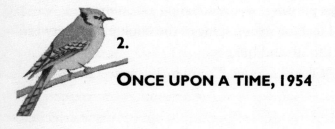

2.

ONCE UPON A TIME, 1954

Once upon a time, I could walk and run.

For me, there's a huge mountain in my childhood. Everything that happened – all that I was before the mountain – is once upon a time.

Does everyone have a mountain in their lives, a before and after?

The mountain fills my sky and I will never cross its peak, never go back to that other time, before I got polio. But I *remember* everything.

My legs moved perfectly then. I didn't have to think about what they did. If I felt like running, I ran. If I wanted to get to the top of a tree, I climbed. In my memories, I ran ahead of Mom everywhere we went. "Slow down, Pauline," she'd call behind me. Even then, she never spoke French to anyone, except to

Grand-mère. Not in Don Mills. She wanted to belong.

Henry lived next door. He was better than a brother or a cousin because we never fought. My parents liked him too, especially Dad.

A year older than me, Henry was bigger and his legs longer than mine. He led the way wherever we went. On rainy days we built dams in the sewers and recreated big storms. We played that our world, Don Mills, was in danger of being flooded and washed away. But no! Henry and I would knock out those dams. We were heroes, saving the world and everyone in it.

Billy Talon and Stuart O'Connor – they lived further down Chelsea Street – always wanted to play with us. But it was way better without them; they wrecked our play with their wrestling and fighting. Henry and I were a team: a dazzling duo. So, if Stuart and Billy followed us as we played, Henry would make the gesture with his thumb. *Go away*: you can't be part of our brave deeds.

On sunny days our favorite game was chasing bad guys off our street. My father even made wooden stickhorses for us to ride. I chose the red one. Henry's was blue. We rode up and down the green lawns saving old Mrs. Hankenstein, the widow, or Mrs. Dickson with the twins who cried all the time. I was allowed to run as many lawns as I had years. I counted them – one, two, three, four, five, six – as Henry and I chased all the bad guys off our street, keeping Don Mills safe.

One, two, three, four, five, six … then came the summer I turned seven.

For several days before my birthday, I felt lightheaded and tired. The morning of my seventh birthday, I was hot and my throat hurt, but I didn't want to tell my mother, because it was my birthday. Henry knocked at the front door, calling on me to come out and play. I splashed cold, cold water on my face and followed him outside.

Henry suggested we chase bad guys on our horses. I didn't say anything. I felt sick. I dragged out my red horse and began to ride. Because it was my birthday, Henry let me take the lead. I rode dizzily. Strangely, the lawns had turned into a mountain and I was struggling up toward a distant peak, getting hotter and hotter. I had to prod my horse to keep going. Maybe I was too close to the sun. Maybe it would burn us up.

A terrible hurting went right through me, beginning in my head, right down to my feet, and then …

I fell off my horse and lay on the ground, feeling like a deflated balloon, waiting for Henry to find me and help me.

He did. He stood over me, upside-down, laughing as if I were playing a joke. "Wow. How'd you fall like that?" he asked.

I didn't answer. He seemed a long, long way away, on the other side of a mountain.

Henry must have sensed something was wrong,

for he put his hand on my forehead, just like our mothers would.

"Hey, Paulie. You're really hot. Are you okay?"

I shook my head. No. I wasn't okay. I'd never felt sick like this before. I'd had chicken pox in the spring, but this was way worse.

Henry ran to get my dad. It must have been a Saturday because Dad was home, cutting the grass. I heard the buzz of the lawn mower stop ... there was a long silence ... and then I saw the shiny top of Dad's bald head bobbing toward me as he ran behind Henry.

Scared and confused, I lay on the seventh lawn away from home, aching like crazy, my red horse fallen on the green grass beside me. I was scared and confused because I felt too sick to get up.

Dad knelt beside me. I could see flecks of fear in his eyes when I whispered, "Can you carry me home, Dad?"

• • •

I went to bed and slept right through until the next morning. My curtains were open and sunlight flooded my room, rousing me. It was hotter than yesterday, and my throat felt like I'd swallowed burning rocks. I had to get to the bathroom.

With an effort I sat up dizzily and swung my legs, letting my feet drop to the floor. I started to walk across the room, but instead toppled against my dresser, my left leg buckling under me.

Something was the matter with my left leg. It didn't want to move or hold me up. I tried to drag myself toward my open door, holding onto the dresser, but it was too hard. I collapsed on the floor.

"Mom!" I called out weakly. "Dad!"

They came running into my room. The bright yellow daisies on my mother's housecoat were bobbing and swaying crazily.

"I can't move my leg," I said.

A look of helpless panic came over my mother's face. Even my dad couldn't hide his fear as he immediately cradled me in his arms and swept me off the floor. "Go call Dr. Shinobu," he ordered Mom into action. "This isn't a flu."

She ran and phoned our family doctor. Dr. Shinobu seemed to appear within minutes to check me over. Then the three of them left my room and I could hear their urgent voices out in the hallway. Mom came back in my room and yanked a few clothes from my drawers, helped me get dressed, then packed a bag for me. "Dr. Shinobu says we should get you to a hospital for some tests," she explained in a tight voice. "Don't worry, dear. You're going to be all right."

Dad carried me outside and put me in the back seat of the car. We drove downtown to the hospital. A quiet fear rode in the car with us and though they wouldn't name it, I knew its name.

Everyone was terrified of polio. We called it the summer plague. The summer before had been the worst epidemic in years. People told stories at school, at church, at the corner store, everywhere. Someone always knew someone who had it. One of Dad's best friends at work lost his wife and new baby to it. And my mother had taught students at the university who caught polio and never returned. Magazines showed pictures, too, pictures of sad-looking kids lying sick and helpless in those iron lungs. A huge poster showing one of those kids hung in the waiting room of Dr. Shinobu's office, and I cowered with fear beside my mother whenever I had to look at it. Those poor kids! Locked inside those tin-can prisons.

Dr. Shinobu had kept his voice quiet in the hallway after he checked me over, but I heard two words, plain as day: *paralysis* and *breathing*.

Buildings and statues sped by outside the car window. Dully I looked at the signs, trying to read them. I loved reading, maybe because I read so much with my mother. I was counting the days until grade two started in September. Only ten days left. I *had* to get better for school. I was the best reader in my class. When Dad pulled up in front of a big building downtown, I looked up to see several words above the wide front doors. The first word was long and unfamiliar. It began with "H." But the last three words, I read easily. I sounded them out and felt a tremendous sense of relief wash over me. I guessed at the first, long word: "Hospital for Sick Children." This was the place that would get me better for the first day of school.

But in the hospital, the doctor took one look at me and growled at the nurses, "This child needs a spinal tap. Get her up to the infectious ward. I hope there's a space left."

I overheard the nurses explain the spinal tap to my parents – the need to draw out some of my spinal fluid to test for polio. No one bothered explaining anything to me. I was just a kid. But I heard the nurses warn my parents that I'd feel a sharp pinch when the needle went in. Ha! They'd have been more honest if they'd said, "It's going to feel like a knife in her back." And even if they had, I could hardly jump up and run away. By then, I couldn't even crawl. Already I was so weak and achy all over, I could barely roll over for them when they wheeled me, alone, into a little room. They tucked me into a fetal position on my side, exposing my back. When that needle stabbed into my spine, I screamed for all I was worth.

Out in the hallway again, I saw my mother. Her eyes had a new, wild look. Had she heard my scream? Why did she let them do that to me? She looked as terrified as I was beginning to feel. Two nurses had to hold her back as they wheeled me by. "No, Mrs. Teal. You can't kiss her or touch her. She's highly contagious."

They wheeled me into an elevator, down a hall

and into a ward which had a long hall with glass walls showing many rooms. Each room was big enough to hold four children. They wheeled me into one and stopped. I saw the tin-can prison, the one I'd seen in those pictures and the poster in the doctor's office. It was an empty iron lung – it was for me. Why did I need one? I could still breathe, couldn't I?

There were three other iron lungs in the room. They made me think of coffins, only there were real live girls inside each one. Just their heads stuck out near the glass wall, and I saw the reflection of their eyes, watching me, in the little mirrors fixed above their heads.

The other girls didn't talk to me. We were too sick to talk. Besides, the room was noisy with the sound of the bellows sucking air in and out of the airtight iron lungs. *Whoosh, whoosh.* "Sixteen times a minute," one of the nurses explained loudly. "The iron lung forces air in and out of your lungs. It will do the breathing for you until your muscles work again."

The kind nurse who explained this had red hair and freckles, and looking at her I thought of Anne of Green Gables, from my mother's favorite book. "The iron lung will keep you alive," Nurse Anne continued.

I shook my head, terrified, sure it was a coffin.

"You're lucky," the other nurse interrupted impatiently. She was young too, but she had enormous bulging eyes and appeared to have no hair beneath her starched white cap. I called her Nurse Toad in my mind, for I was afraid of toads. "There's an epidemic. This is the last iron lung available in the hospital. The next child who comes in here will be out in the hall without one."

Nurse Anne ignored her and continued to explain how the iron lung worked as she opened up one end and slid out my bed. Then they lifted me onto it and pushed me inside. Only my head stuck out the hole, through a rubber collar. They clamped the bed shut and turned it on.

"You'll feel better soon," Nurse Anne said with a smile before she turned away to help another girl.

Whoosh, whoosh, went the bellows. In and out. *Whoosh, whoosh.*

I looked around me at the other girls. Did I look like them?

Someone in the room was crying. Or was it … me?

Whoosh, whoosh. I could feel a strange pressure on my chest as the air was forced out and then drawn into my lungs. In and out. Slowly, amazingly, I began to feel a little better. I'd had no idea I'd been fighting to breathe.

Whoosh, whoosh. In and out. Tired. I was so, so tired.

Finally I slept.

3.

DREAMING WITH
TANTE MARIE, 1959

First thing I do every morning when I get up is check the calendar. I'm counting the days until Tante Marie's arrival.

I write B a letter. He lives up north so I haven't seen him since we both left the rehabilitation hospital four years ago. He's still a great fan of Tante Marie's and will be happy for me that she's coming. I also finish two more books from the pile to make the time pass quickly, but I read them in secret so my mother won't know. Last year, the summer I turned eleven, we had a family reunion in Québec. My two aunts called me spoiled and self-centered, thinking I wouldn't understand when they whispered *gâtée* in French. Maybe they're right. I don't care.

I can't wait to see Tante Marie. She never speaks a word against me, not in any language.

My father brings Tante Marie and Grand-mère home from Union Station. My mother has welcoming hugs and kisses for Grand-mère, but when she turns to Tante Marie, she freezes and pulls herself back stiffly. She's the ice queen.

Tante Marie kisses her cheeks anyway and asks how she is. "Agathe. *Ça va bien?*"

I am so excited. Tante Marie is here. I want to jump up and down.

My turn! Tante Marie gathers me close and calls me beautiful. "*Ma belle.*" She kisses both my cheeks and she is soothing and electric, all at the same time. I feel special. Even the scent of her perfume embraces me. "You've grown so tall. Come, get your coat and we'll walk and try to get caught up."

My mother protests, "Outside? It's too icy; she could fall."

"*Ridicule!*" Tante Marie laughs and gently brushes my perfectly bobbed, chin-length hair back from my face, behind my ears. "Pauline can't stay in all day."

My heart races. Mom and Marie have started, like they always do. If they don't fight over me, it will be over Grand-mère, or what we'll eat for dinner.

"What do you know about it, Marie? She's my daughter and you should mind your own business."

"I'm still her aunt and whether you like it or not

she's my business. Besides, a total stranger could see how you've got her cooped up in here ..."

"*Mes filles!*" Grand-mère scolds them from the living room where Dad is settling her in a comfortable chair. She shakes a bony finger at her bickering daughters. "*Ça suffit.*"

But they can't stop, not even with Grand-mère as referee.

"She needs to walk and get outdoors. Books aren't enough, Agathe."

"Polio crippled her legs, not her mind."

"Agatha!" My father leaves Grand-mère's side. He's angry; he rarely raises his voice against my mother. "She just got here. At least let them go for a walk."

My mother crosses her arms over her chest and glares at her sister. "Pauline doesn't like to walk at this hour. Ask her yourself."

My mother's right. I have to walk every day, to strengthen my muscles. But on weekdays I walk in the morning, after kids go to school, and on weekends I walk when it's dark and I don't have to endure curious stares.

Feeling reckless in Tante Marie's company, I do up my coat and shuffle out the door without looking at my mother. "I just got a letter from B. It's in my pocket. You can read it while we walk," I say to my aunt.

Tante Marie holds the door and follows me. "We'll

be back in time for drinks," she laughs over her shoulder, just before the screen door clicks shut. "We'll run the whole way back."

Outside, I lurch slowly down the street while Tante Marie reads B's letter. We pass Henry's house, the Martins', Mrs. Hankenstein's and the Talons'. I keep my head down. I don't want to see them if they're gawking. I walk like Frankenstein. My left leg is short and thin and I wear a metal brace around it, up to my thigh, to support me as I walk.

My father says Don Mills was the post-war dream for happy families. Everything along these wide streets, from the big backyards to the central library, was carefully planned. Everything but polio epidemics.

"That boy," says Tante Marie proudly, finishing B's letter. "I'm so glad he found a high school that would accept him."

"You're going too fast, Tante Marie," I pant, stopping to catch my breath, seeking a dry patch of asphalt so my crutches won't slip. "You know I can't run. I never will."

"What makes you talk like that? Look at B. He's got braces on both legs, yet he's going to a regular school." She laughs, holding up B's letter. "He'll show them. He's already Captain of the Debating Team. And look at me. Not one of my sisters believes I'll ever be a successful artist. They hate my sculptures, but I dream, one day, my work — it will be in the Louvre."

She gestures dramatically toward the east, in the direction of Paris. "Everybody's got a dream to keep them going. You too, *n'est-ce pas, chérie?*"

I haven't shared my dream with anyone. In my mind, I see our new backyard rink, the ice hard and gleaming. Here's my chance to share my dream with Tante Marie pointing at a distant horizon. Her cheeks are so brilliant, they almost match the blazing red of her beret. No one wears a red beret in Don Mills.

"One day … I want to skate with my father," I say softly.

"Ahh. Such a wonderful dream." She smiles. "Before I go back to Montréal, I will do something for you about that dream."

Tante Marie is the only adult I know who keeps her promises. She helped me once when I was desperate, and I know she will help me again.

Walking home, I see Henry playing road hockey with Stuart and Billy. They are his two best friends now. They live at the other end of Chelsea — why do they have to play up here? They wear the same blue, shiny jackets as Henry, and I suspect they are on the same hockey team. Henry stands in goal and is the only one facing me. He doesn't gawk, but he can't be paying attention, for the other boys yell "Score!" twice in the minute it takes us to walk by.

"Hi, Pauline."

It takes me by surprise and I stop. Why is Henry

saying hello? Does he hope for an invitation to skate on our new rink? Never!

Stuart and Billy turn around and stare at Tante Marie and me.

Are they gawking? No. They're just looking.

Tante Marie is looking at me too, waiting. I should say hi. There's another reason for Henry saying hello. Tante Marie is incredibly beautiful. People always like her.

The "Hi" starts in my throat — and stops.

I still have to walk — lurch — the last hundred yards to the front door. I nod my head stiffly.

"Come on, Henry. Let's play," Stuart says, shooting the ball to Billy.

I walk. I wish I could hold my head up, but I have to watch carefully for ice. It would be awful if I fell, sprawling in front of them. My face, I'm sure, has turned brighter than Tante Marie's beret.

Then I remember Tante Marie's promise. She is going to make my dream come true. I won't fall in front of these boys. I won't! I can do this — and more! For the first time in four years, hope flexes its muscle as if rising from a long and troubled sleep, rising like a bird on a strong breeze, soaring up there just like the dreams of every other kid in Don Mills.

4.

IN THE HOSPITAL FOR SICK CHILDREN, 1954

The nurse was right. I was lucky. I had the last available iron lung.

For over a week I lay feverish, sleeping most of the time – but breathing. A little mirror was attached to the iron lung, over my head. Whenever I woke up I could see, in that mirror, whatever was happening in the hallway behind me.

There seemed to be a constant traffic of beds coming in, piling up in the hallway, waiting. Nurses scurrying back and forth. In the days and then weeks that passed, I twice saw a bed leave from that hallway. Both times the sheet was pulled up over a small body, up over a face. I knew what that meant. I knew it was another kid, just like me.

Now I was awake most of the day, thinking. With all that time to think, I'd figured out the reason I was here, sick in the hospital. It was because of the red horse. If I had had the blue horse, it would have been Henry to get polio instead of me.

The strange thing about polio was that it affected the nerves that told my muscles to move. But it didn't attack the nerves that told me what hurt.

And I hurt.

The nurses were tired and busy. They seemed to run from one bed to another, checking, feeding, cleaning. There were little round plastic windows in the sides of the iron lung that they could open to check for sores or clean me or move me around.

The last time I spoke, I asked for help. My legs were aching terribly, but I was unable to move them or relieve the pain in any way. The paralysis had spread up to my neck. I lay unable to move my head, struggling to swallow, feeling a searing pain in my legs. Unfortunately, Nurse Toad was on duty. I could hear her croaking as she attended the girl next to me. If only Nurse Anne would come. I waited and waited. But my legs. What was happening to my legs? I couldn't see them, but it felt like something horrible was sawing and burning through them.

"Please, help!" I moaned. "It hurts!" My voice was weak and I could barely whisper.

Nurse Toad moved over me quicker than a storm

cloud. "Who do you think you are? Of course you hurt. You've got polio. Everybody in here is hurting. At least you're alive. At least you're in an iron lung. You've got a chance to live in an iron lung. But if you don't stop that hollering, I'll take you out of it and give it to one of those poor children in the hallway. And believe me I will!"

I knew she would, too. Her eyes were bloated with anger.

I swallowed back my terror. It was dangerous to talk in here. And I didn't want to lose my iron lung. I didn't want to end up with the sheet pulled over my face.

So … I stopped talking.

In those first weeks, while we were considered contagious, my parents weren't allowed in. After a while, when the hallway cleared of beds, they were allowed to stand outside the glass wall behind me. I saw them in the little mirror. I knew they couldn't help me. All I had on my side was this noisy, *whooshing* iron lung. The best way to stay safe – and alive – was to keep quiet. The iron lung was not a coffin; it was a cocoon.

It wasn't hard to stay silent. The muscles in my throat were affected anyway, and I was very tired. So I concentrated on breathing. There was a big clock on the wall and I counted the *whooshes.* Sixteen a minute.

More weeks passed slowly. My parents were allowed to visit on Sundays. They could stand outside the glass wall and wave or send messages with Nurse Anne if she was on duty. I counted Sundays now. One, two, three, four, five, six, seven, eight, nine, ten, eleven, twelve. Swallowing got easier. I could nod and shake my head at them, although I still couldn't move my arms or hands or legs.

Christmas came. My parents stood outside the glass wall and waved at me. I watched them in the mirror. Nurse Anne brought me their gift, a new teddy bear. He was brown with a bright red bow around his neck, and I could tell by looking at him, he'd be soft and cuddly. If only she'd lay him against my cheek. But I kept quiet, even with Nurse Anne. I tried to tell her with my eyes.

"Your parents brought you a gift. Don't let yourself get too attached to him," she warned softly. "You won't be allowed to keep …"

She stopped talking. She snuggled his soft face against mine. "He's giving you a kiss," she said. "Merry Christmas, Pauline."

He smelled like apple cider, spiced with cinnamon, the way my mother made it. He smelled of home.

"He wants to stay close to you," Nurse Anne said. "Here." She hooked him over the mirror so that he sat looking directly at me.

When my parents left, I felt like there was a big hole inside me. I wanted to go home and see my room. I imagined our Christmas tree. It would be a pine, filling the house with its fresh, wintry, forest smell. I was sick of the antiseptic smell of the hospital ward and the metal air of the iron lung.

Then I looked up and saw my bear, sitting on the little mirror. I liked his bright red bow and black button eyes. I didn't feel quite so lonely.

"I'll call you Henry," I told him silently. "That's my best friend's name." It was nice to have a friend to talk with again.

And Christmas wasn't over.

Later that afternoon, I got another present, a different kind. I wriggled the toes on my left foot. Nurse Anne was changing the bedpan under my bed and must have seen the movement.

She stood up, nearly dropping the bedpan. "Oh, Pauline! You moved your toes," she said with excitement. "Let me go get the doctor."

It didn't take her long to find him and bring him into the ward. He smiled, encouraging me. "Can you show me that movement? Try to move your toes again, Pauline," he said.

I did. Months of nothing … and now I could move my toes again!

The next day, the doctor came back and told me I was going to come out of the iron lung for a short period to see if I could breathe on my own. I was scared. My eyes must have shouted my fear.

"Relax," said the doctor kindly. "Don't you worry.

We'll put you back in the iron lung the second you show signs of having trouble. But if you do okay, we'll take you out every day for longer and longer periods. And then one day, when you're in the clear, you might be able to go to a rehabilitation hospital, maybe even home. How does that sound?"

I didn't speak … but I nodded.

They turned off the bellows, opened the iron lung and slid me out. My lungs kept moving. I was alive, breathing on my own. Excitement must have shone in my eyes because the doctor and Nurse Anne smiled and clapped their hands. I could breathe on my own! I didn't need the iron lung. And I could wriggle my left toes!

I felt great hope. "Don't you worry," I told Henry, "we'll be home soon."

5.

CHRISTMAS WITH TANTE MARIE, 1959

We celebrate Christmas on Christmas Eve. It is the only tradition my mother keeps from her childhood in Québec. But before gifts are opened in the early hours of the morning, my mother, Grand-mère and Tante Marie go to celebrate midnight mass at church.

My father and I stay home and play poker. He teaches me a new game, Fiery Cross, and I imagine a disaster.

"What if Grand-mère slips and falls and dies at church? Would Mom blame it on Tante Marie?"

Dad turns over a seven of clubs in the middle of the cross and shrugs his shoulders. "Probably."

In my hand, I have two black fives, a jack of hearts, and the seven and eight of clubs. "Even after communion and she's filled with all that forgiveness stuff?"

"Yup. Even after that."

"What's her problem?"

"What's yours? You got a bad hand?" He turns over another card, revealing a nine of clubs.

"I'd never forgive her if she wouldn't let me see Tante Marie. She wouldn't do that would she? Why doesn't she like Tante Marie?"

"Relax, Pauline. Leave that worrying stuff to your mother. She does enough for the three of us."

He turns over a nine of hearts. I close up my cards and glare at him. Talk to me! He sighs and raises his bushy black eyebrows at me. "We've been through this, Pauline. Accept it. The sun sets in the west and your mother doesn't like her youngest sister. Never has, never will. It's pure sibling rivalry. Remember Joseph's brothers in the Bible? Some siblings sell each other into slavery. Whoa, Nelly," he interrupts himself, beaming. "This is a winning hand. Any bets?"

He has to turn over one more card. If it's the six of clubs, I'll have a flush. Pretty good. Dad's probably right. I don't want to think anymore about this sibling thing. Shouldn't sisters and brothers love each other? I'm glad I don't have to worry about it.

"I'll bet the morning dishes."

"You're on." He turns over another card in the cross. It's the six of clubs.

"Flush!" I say, triumphantly, fanning out my hand. "I win."

"That's good, Paulie. But not good enough to beat dear old Dad." He fans out his hand. "Full house. Three nines and a pair of sixes. He, he, he, no dishes for me."

"I know you cheat, Dad." I pound him lightly on the arm.

"Ho, ho, ho, you'll never know."

"Grow up, Dad," I groan. "One more game. I deal."

But they're home. We hear the sound of the door slamming and angry voices in the front hallway.

"I'll drive from now on," my mother says as they enter the room. "If you're going to drive that fast, you might as well kill us all right here and now." She's holding Grand-mère by the elbow, fussing over her. I know Grand-mère doesn't understand English. But she doesn't need to; she understands her daughters.

Grand-mère swats at my mother, telling her to stop complaining. She's glad Marie was driving because they got home faster. She can't wait to open her gifts. She smiles at me, then Dad. "*Joyeux Noël.*"

"Joyous Noel," Dad says in his awful French. Then, with a mocking sternness, "Emphasis on joy, girls. So no fighting on Christmas. Sit down and I'll hand out your presents. They're great this year. Believe me, we know. Pauline opened and rewrapped everything while you were out."

"Dad!" I laugh and pound him again on the arm.

"If you keep hitting me like that, I won't be able to hand out the presents."

Tante Marie laughs and joins me on the window seat. "I know you wouldn't do that, *chérie*." She arcs her arm around me and I relax against her, feeling the warm circle of happiness that I only feel with her.

Dad reads the names on the gifts, passing them out, one by one. Pretty soon I have a little pile. I start with the obvious: the hard, rectangular ones from my mother.

I groan inside but I find a way to thank her for the books. "*Heidi*. Looks good. I'll start it next week." The second one, I really wonder about. "*Presidents of the United States*?"

I let the books slide, unwanted, to the floor as I open Grand-mère's gift. It's an album of her favorite singer, Edith Piaf, the songbird of Paris during the war years. At family gatherings, Grand-mère starts humming one favorite song, and then my mother and my aunts join in, united for once, dreamy eyes for the last phrase, something like *mon cœur qui bat*.

"*Fantastique, Maman*," Tante Marie laughs, jumping off the window seat. She takes the record from me. "It's our tradition, Pauline. You'll have to learn her big song so you can sing with us."

"That one you always sing?"

She walks to the record player, already humming

it before she puts the needle down.

"What's the last line mean?" I ask.

"It means your heart is beating. It means love is alive in you. One of these days, some boy will come along … and you'll be singing it with the rest of us."

I feel like saying, "A crippled heart? What boy would ever be interested in me?"

But it's Christmas. Tante Marie is here, arms linked with Grand-mère, who is singing in her sweet, warbly soprano. My mother is linked to Grand-mère's other side, singing alto harmony. I'm happy listening to them sing. When the song's over, I reach for Dad's present. I rip the paper off a big box. Inside it, there's a smaller one, and inside it, an even smaller one. Nesting boxes. In the very center are two tiny, incredible tickets. I scream with excitement.

"Oh, Dad. Two tickets for the Leafs game at the Gardens. January 28th. Wow!" I jiggle up and down on the window seat. I feel like jumping up and doing cartwheels to the front hall.

"Isn't it damp and cold in the Gardens?" my mother says nervously.

"You worry too much," Dad says. "We'll dress warm and take a blanket."

My mother bites her lip.

In a daze, I watch everybody open their gifts. I'm going to watch a Leafs game at the Gardens! What could be better?

I shake my head. This has to be because of Tante Marie. I love when she comes. I start to come out of my daze. But what about Tante Marie's gift? Has she forgotten about her promise?

Tante Marie is standing beside the Christmas tree. From a hidden place behind the tinsel-strewn branches she pulls out two hockey sticks, each tied with a red velvet ribbon. One she hands to my dad, the other, winking, to me.

My mother is holding the gift I've given her. The glass ball sits in the palm of her hand. A tiny nativity scene is encased in water, and she has just shaken it. Snow drifts through the water, falling on baby Jesus and the animals around him, while she asks faintly, "What will Pauline do with a hockey stick?"

Tante Marie laughs as if my mother has told a funny joke. "She'll play hockey on the new rink, of course. Don't you still have her old wheelchair?"

"You can't be serious. That wheelchair won't have any traction on the ice. She'll tip right out!"

But my father spins Tante Marie around, laughing. "That's a great idea. Why didn't I think of it? There's nothing I'd like better than to play hockey with Pauline."

I've never held a hockey stick before. I take it in my hands. It feels big and strange. I swing my legs over the edge of the window seat and press the blade of the stick against the blue-and-red braided rug that covers our floor. The red velvet ribbon falls off and without thinking, I flick it with the blade.

How many hockey games have I watched on TV? Yet this is the first time I've held a hockey stick or tried to shoot like my idols. I feel a surge of power as I watch the ribbon sail through the air and land beside Tante Marie.

"You're a natural," Dad beams at me. "You're going to have a great shot. You've already got your wrists into it."

Without looking at my mother, Tante Marie picks up the red ribbons and begins to tie them together.

But I peek at my mother. A strand of straight, brown hair has fallen loose from the tight bun at the back of her head. It hangs like a limp, broken wing on one shoulder. She looks like she's at a funeral, not a Christmas party. Her face is creased with fear and it makes my stomach hurt to look at her. Why doesn't she ever believe in me?

Tante Marie saves the moment. Playfully, she finishes tying the red ribbons together and places them, a bright *couronne,* in Grand-mère's white curls. Grand-mère tisks as if Marie is being foolish. "Tisk, tisk." But when Grand-mère stands and looks at herself in the large mirror over our sofa, she looks young and girlish, like a hopeful bride.

Grand-mère catches me looking at her in the mirror. Unexpectedly, her face unwraps with laughter.

6.

THE HOUSE OF HORRORS, JANUARY 1955

I left the Hospital for Sick Children soon after I could breathe without the iron lung. It was a wonderful day, and a terrible day. They took Henry from me and burned him. They were afraid he might carry the polio virus from the ward. No personal items were allowed out.

Alone, I was taken by ambulance to a big old house that had been converted into a rehabilitation hospital.

My parents met me briefly as I arrived. My mother showered me with kisses. She held my hand but I couldn't hug her back or hold onto her like I wanted. I still couldn't move. Dad had brought me my favorite drink, an Orange Crush in a little brown bottle. Where was a bottle opener? I was dying to taste it, the sweet orange liquid that would fizz down my throat.

But the new nurse, Nurse Wilson, quickly took over. She held out her hand to take my Orange Crush and in a sickly sweet voice she said, "Oh no, we can't have that. We'll save it for when she's better."

Perplexed, Dad looked at me. My eyes were filling up. There was something about Nurse Wilson that reminded me of Nurse Toad. Her eyes were small, but they looked just as mean and uncaring as they flickered over my unmoving body.

Dad didn't give the bottle to her. "I don't see why she couldn't have a little sip. It's her favorite drink."

Nurse Wilson looked sternly from my father to my mother. "I've worked in this hospital for ten years. I'm the head nurse. I've known some of these polios to choke on pop."

My mother looked nervous. My heart sank. I knew Nurse Wilson would turn into a witch. Just like Nurse Toad, the moment my parents were gone, her fake syrupy voice would harden. I'd be just one more polio causing her too much work.

Nurse Wilson pressed her point. "You wouldn't want to do that to your daughter after she's survived so much, would you, Mom?"

Slowly, my mother shook her head … and Nurse Wilson took my Orange Crush.

How could my mother believe her? They burned Henry. I had nothing. All I wanted was my pop!

I'd lost half my body weight. I felt like Gretel, that skin-and-bones orphan, waiting to be fed to the fire by Witch Wilson. I could taste it; I wanted it so badly, one cool, sweet sip of my Orange Crush.

I never saw that Orange Crush again.

My parents said goodbye and I was carried on a stretcher into my new home. The ward held eight children, different ages, but all lying in cribs. My first impression was that I had come to a zoo, but I was immediately corrected. It was going to be something worse.

"Welcome to the House of Horrors," the boy opposite me called as soon as Nurse Wilson left.

She'd installed me in a crib and pulled up the barred side. It would prevent me from falling out – or escaping – if I ever moved again.

I lifted my head and stared at the boy for a long moment. What did he mean? Whose side was he on?

"Don't you talk, or what?" he said.

I looked around the room. Everybody was watching us.

"That's okay," he said. "I'll talk for you. I'm almost ten, though I'm so small you'd never know it. My name's Bernardo. You can call me B."

As if on cue, they all called out their names, introducing themselves. On the boys' side were Frank, Philip and Stan. Beside me were Janet, Mary and Lorna. I looked over at B. He seemed to be the leader.

"That's Witch Wilson who brought you in. Head

nurse. Everyone's afraid of her. The other nurses are nice, but you got to be careful of Witch Wilson. She's bad news. She's in with Nurse Fredericks in physio. They're like this –" He twisted two fingers together. "Mother Mary and the Holy Ghost help you if you get Nurse Fredericks for physio. If you scream in physio, Fredericks tells the Witch. Oh, mamma mia," he moaned, shaking his head. "I don't know which witch is worse."

Everybody laughed. A smile lifted the corners of B's mouth. "Get it? Which witch is worse?"

I smiled. There were no noisy iron lungs here. It felt so strange to be in a quiet room with kids talking to each other. Almost normal. Suddenly I realized … it felt great.

I thought about talking, about saying hello to the other kids. But hospitals were strange places. You never really knew if you were safe or not. Better to watch and wait.

"My arms and hands are coming back," he continued. "Soon as I can walk, I'll be out o' here. But till I go, I'll help you out. We help each other. It's us against them, right, guys?"

"Right," everyone chorused.

All this time, since getting polio on my birthday, I'd wondered what I'd done wrong. I was sure God was mad at me. I was being punished for choosing the red horse.

And now, Bernardo! He was a gift, filling the empty space in my life that had been left when they took away Henry. For the first time in four months, I thought maybe God wasn't mad at me anymore.

Over the next weeks, I watched and waited. I didn't talk.

I learned quickly. The doctors and nurses were busy but nice enough. However, just as Bernardo had warned, it was dangerous to have a problem if Witch Wilson was around. Janet, the girl beside me, wore a heavy brace at night. One morning she was crying because it had been fastened too tight. I watched her pull and pull at the leather strap, unable to get it loose. Could Nurse Wilson please take it off? Nurse Wilson plunked Janet's food on the table where Janet and Bernardo were supposed to sit and eat their meals. But Janet was stuck in her crib in the brace, pulling at the strap. Witch Wilson went about the room, feeding those of us who were paralyzed in our cribs, bringing bedpans and clean clothes. She finished everybody else before she finally stood beside Janet and gave an enormous yank on the strap. Janet cried out with pain, but she was free. "Hmmphh. It's about time you learned to get that off yourself," Witch Wilson said coldly. Then she turned away and whisked Janet's food tray from the little table. "Breakfast is over."

After she left, Bernardo pulled out a piece of toast and jam for Janet. The red jam was almost as bright as the mark around her leg.

"One good thing," he said. "You didn't wet your pants." Cynthia laughed so hard, she nearly did.

Bernardo turned to me. "You ain't seen nothing yet. Wait till someone messes their bed." He told me Witch Wilson punished kids who messed their beds, but I didn't believe him. Other nurses, even Nurse Toad, just cleaned up accidents. Kids with polio couldn't help it. It was the nurse's job to change the sheets. Not Witch Wilson. She took it as a sign of the worst disobedience.

One morning I saw fear in Bernardo's eyes – and then I smelled his problem.

Witch Wilson was already in the ward, pushing the trolley with our food trays. Those who could sit up and feed themselves got theirs first.

"Someone's dirtied their bed. Some lazy child here couldn't wait." She left the trolley and stomped through the ward, from bed to bed. She stopped beside B's bed like a wolf cornering her prey.

"So it's you!" she sneered triumphantly. "You think I believe you can't control yourself? You think I've got nothing better to do than clean your sheets?"

She took the brakes off the wheels under his crib. Down at the end of the ward was a deep closet. Deep enough to push a crib inside and close the doors. Deep and dark.

I'm sure she cackled as she closed the doors on B.

"At least we won't have to look at you all day. And if I hear one whimper out of you, you'll be sleeping there tonight!"

I felt terrible for Bernardo. He was always the one to tell stories and sing songs at night, after lights out. Everybody loved B, so we started singing his favorite songs softly while Stan, whose crib was near the door, kept lookout. Witch Wilson let B out of the closet after lunch. She wouldn't let him eat, though. He had missed breakfast and the hot noon meal, but everybody who could had saved something for him.

B kept his eyes down until Witch Wilson left the ward.

Then he sat up.

"Hey, everybody. I'm back!" he crowed.

Frank, the boy whose crib was beside Bernardo's, threw him some crackers; Janet, an apple.

"Thanks," B said, munching hungrily. "We'll show her tonight. Right?"

B reminded me of my Tante Marie. I missed her terribly. She was away finishing her art studies in Paris and I hadn't seen her in all these months I'd been sick with polio. She had no idea the trouble I was in. How could she? I couldn't write her. I didn't talk. And my parents only saw what Nurse Wilson was like on visiting day. But I knew Tante Marie would have seen right through her. She was full of rebellion, just like B.

B told us his plan and we cheered.

That evening after supper was served, things started dropping. Anyone who could, dropped a glass or cutlery or food. Anything we could push out of our cribs and onto the floor was pushed, especially juice and bowls of strawberry Jello.

The ward was a total mess. The cleaning woman didn't come in until morning, and the doctor was about to make evening rounds.

It was a protest.

"What's going on in here? Nurse Wilson?" the doctor asked as he entered our ward. His feet made ripping noises as he tried to unstick himself from the sugar-coated floor. Nurse Wilson stood behind him. Her face turned the same color as the gelatinous glop under her white shoes.

No one said a word. But the doctor ordered Nurse Wilson to clean it up.

And we watched her scrub, smiling small, quiet smiles of victory at each other.

7.

CHRISTMAS MORNING, 1959

Dad gently shakes me awake. "Shh. Want to go out on the rink?"

He presses a warning finger against his lips. "Mom's still asleep."

I nod vigorously.

"Dress warm," he whispers. "Leave your brace off and I'll carry you outside."

How warmly? I think of how the kids look when they pull toboggans down the street on a snowy day. They are so bundled up, they walk like stuffed crepes. I pull on two pairs of tights, flannel-lined pants and three sweaters. With my long coat, it should be enough.

Thankfully, my bedroom is by the side door. Dad comes back, scoops me up and we're outside before my mother can turn over in her sleep. "I put oil on the garage door so it doesn't squeak," he whispers. "We'll prove to her there's nothing to worry about."

He's put a folding lawn chair beside the rink. He sits me on it and heads for the garage. Feeling like a thief stealing a risky moment, I clench my hands as he opens the door. For once it swings up silently, and he disappears for a moment inside, then reappears, bringing my new hockey stick and my old wheelchair.

"Cold?" he whispers when he tucks me under an old blanket in the wheelchair.

"No. Come on, Dad. Before she wakes up."

He tilts the wheelchair back to get the front wheels over the hard snowbank edging the rink, and I look up to see Henry watching from his window. I'm so happy, I wave at him.

I feel a strong urgency to get on the rink before my mother wakes up. There's no time to worry about Henry.

I'm on the rink!

Cautiously, Dad pushes me forward. "It certainly slides. I wonder how it will do when we try to turn around the goal at the other end."

"Come on, Dad. This is great!"

We start to move across the hard, white ice, getting closer to the other end. I love it. I ignore the numbing cold in my legs. What will happen if we can't turn? Yikes! We'll crash into the fence. Bravely, I hold my hockey stick out in front of me, planning to push off the wooden boards if need be. But the wheelchair makes a wide arc, and now we're behind the goal, now heading up the other side of the rink.

"We did it!" I cry.

"You planning to spear yourself with your stick? Put it down on the ice," Dad orders nervously.

I see his breath, like train smoke, above me as we puff down the ice. I have to lean forward slightly to put the blade of the stick down – it bumps up and down. How do hockey players do this so effortlessly?

It's over before we get around a second time.

"Stop, Will!" My mother's anxious voice loops like a lasso around Dad. She stands at the side door in a blue marshmallow-puffed housecoat, waving us in. "Pauline, you could hurt yourself. This is too dangerous." She clutches her housecoat tightly to her throat.

"No, Dad. No."

But he stops and turns toward her. Face-off.

I know who's going to win. My mother wants to tie rocks to my dream. I will never fly around this rink.

"Will, she could slide right out and she'd have no protection. She hasn't even got her brace on. Please, Will. It's Christmas. I don't want to worry on Christmas." Her voice is a tight, strangling knot.

"All right, Agatha." My father sighs. "But just so you know … it *is* safe. We'll try it another time and she'll wear her brace."

My mother scurries back into the house. I hurl my stick against the sideboards. *Whack!*

In his most soothing voice, Dad tries to calm me down. "We'll go along with her for now. You wait. She just needs to get used to the idea."

He has to turn the wheelchair backward to get off the rink. The wheels get stuck for a second and I hang there, tilted back into cold reality. I'm a cripple. This is a wheelchair. I'll never skate. There's no point to my dream.

Just then Henry's head appears in my line of vision on the other side of the fence, a striped blue-and-yellow toque above his big, stupid grin.

"Merry Christmas!"

"Merry Christmas, Henry," Dad calls back. He pokes me in the shoulder to say something.

No way.

Henry speaks in white puffs of excitement. "Need a goalie? Or a defenseman?"

My dad's so friendly. "Great idea, Henry. Too bad we have to go in for breakfast right now. How about we call you for a game later?"

Henry's smile disappears in disappointment. "Oh."

"But if you've got your skates on now, you can come and skate on our rink if you like."

No way. No way. If I can't, he can't. I start to shake my head back and forth, then my body, thrashing from side to side, one big *no*.

Henry backs away a step, the blue pompom on his toque nodding. I jerk my thumb, the same thing I did to him that time he visited me at the House of Horrors.

Henry gets the same message now as he did then. Only this time I mean it.

Go away.

8.

HENRY'S VISIT TO THE HOUSE OF HORRORS, 1955

After the first awful month in the House of Horrors, we had a welcome change. We had a new, wonderful head nurse most weekends and whenever Witch Wilson took days off.

Bernardo seemed to know about everything – he nicknamed her Nurse Nightingale after a famous nurse he'd heard about.

She laughed when B first called her that, but she didn't try to make him address her by her real name. So it stuck.

My parents brought someone to visit one weekend. It was probably my mother's idea. She hated me not speaking. The more she coaxed, the further inside I went. She had no idea how dangerous it was to talk in here.

"Please, Paulie. Talk to me. Tell me how you are. I don't think you're eating enough and you look so …"

"Now, Mom," Witch Wilson happened to over-hear her. "She's just looking for attention and feeling sorry for herself. I've seen lots of that in here. You're best not to give in to her. She'll talk when she realizes all that silence is not going to get her anything."

My mother looked baffled by this advice. She kept her arm around me but she didn't say anything more.

I didn't care about talking or not talking. My mind was fixed on one thing. I was determined to get out of this place. Somehow, I guessed that my mother couldn't make that happen. The key was getting better. I was going to have to walk again and then they'd let me out.

One Sunday, Nurse Nightingale told me I had visi-tors. "Not just your parents," she said with a teasing grin.

I questioned her with my eyes.

"You'll see who it is. I'll take you over to the win-dow."

Who could it be? I immediately thought of Tante Marie, who had been writing me funny letters every week from Paris.

Nurse Nightingale wheeled my crib over to the window so I could look outside. Our ward was on the main floor and the window looked out onto the side yard. It was winter-white and cold, but Nurse Night-ingale opened the window slightly so my visitor and I could talk.

It wasn't Tante Marie. It was Henry, my best friend, standing right in front of me, waiting beside my parents.

I was surprised.

"I'm sorry about this arrangement," said Nurse Nightingale. "Children under twelve aren't allowed inside."

I could see by the look on Henry's face that he was shocked by my appearance.

"Hi, Pauline."

I lay there like a baby, staring at my once-upon-a-time best friend. Losing my teddy bear had felt like a knife in the back. But here was the real, living Henry. It was too good to believe. Maybe, just maybe, I hadn't lost Henry.

By this time I had full use of my neck and I could wiggle both feet. But that was all. I couldn't sit up, though I desperately wanted to. Behind me in the ward, I suddenly thought about my new best friend, Bernardo, who lay in a crib like I did. On this side of the window lay my hospital world; on the other side was my once-upon-a-time world, separated by a pane of glass.

"Won't you say hello to Henry?" my mother pleaded.

Oh no. It was so obvious: she'd brought Henry to trick me into talking.

"Henry's been wanting to see you," my dad said

gently. "That nice nurse suggested he could come to the window to say hello."

"Henry's come all this way. He's missed a hockey game just to …"

My dad raised his eyebrows at my mother, poking her in the side. "We're going for a little walk, Agatha," he said, putting his arm around my mother and pulling her away. "The kids don't need us adults around." He winked at me.

And then it was just us, alone.

I thought Henry was staring down at the ground for a long time until I raised my head off my pillow enough to see that he was pulling something out of his pocket.

"I brought you my sheriff's badge."

He held up the shiny silver star I knew he treasured. I could see the word SHERIFF on it. We'd played countless games on our red and blue horses, chasing the bad guys. He was always the sheriff, wearing that badge.

I wanted it badly. I could really use it. Maybe if I wore it, I could order Witch Wilson around. Put her in jail, or better yet, chase her away.

I couldn't move my hands to take it. And I still didn't feel safe enough to speak.

But this was Henry. We were all alone, no adults with us. It was tempting, so tempting to say the words to thank him. I could hear them in my mind: "You are my best friend in the whole, wide world."

Henry spoke. "It's okay, Pauline. Your dad told me you're not talking in here. You don't have to say anything."

Henry smiled at me, a smile even shinier than his sheriff's badge.

Maybe I smiled back.

"All the kids on the street are asking about you, waiting for you to come home. After Christmas, we heard you were out of the iron lung. It must have been great to come here."

Here? Great? I stopped smiling. How could I tell him about this place? It was exactly like what B had called it: the House of Horrors.

I must have started crying. I missed Henry. I missed home. I couldn't tell him about this awful place.

Henry didn't know what to do. He reached up and put the sheriff's badge on the window ledge between us.

Automatically, I tried to reach for it. Of course I couldn't; I was paralyzed. But something happened.

My right thumb – just my right thumb – moved. A little jerk.

It looked exactly like Henry's *Go Away* gesture, the one we used to use with Billy Talon and Stuart O'Connor.

A terrible, hurt look spread over Henry's face. He backed away a few steps, shoving his hands in his pockets. He swallowed hard and turned away quickly, almost running in search of my parents.

Nurse Nightingale saw the movement, too. She didn't seem to notice Henry running away. "You moved your thumb, Pauline!" she crowed. "You moved your thumb!"

She walked over and picked up the sheriff's badge from the window ledge. She pinned it happily to my shirt, talking excitedly about what this meant, how she had to call the doctor with the good news.

I didn't feel excited. There was a new, sharp pain – this time in my chest – as if a knife had cut into my heart.

I couldn't run after Henry, and it was too late to call after him.

I had just chased away the best friend in the whole, wide world.

9.

FUNERALS ARE FOR FAMILIES, 1960

Grand-mère gets pneumonia and has to go into hospital. Early one morning in February, Tante Marie phones to tell us the bad news: Grand-mère has died in the night.

From my perch on the window seat, I hear my parents argue all day and into the evening. "Pauline has a cold. She shouldn't travel when she's sick. I'll go to the funeral alone. They'll understand."

"Funerals are for families," Dad argues back. "It's a perfect opportunity for Pauline to see everybody, and you know how fond she is of Marie."

"And look what trouble Marie stirred up at Christmas. She pokes her nose where she shouldn't. Marie's the last person Pauline needs to see."

They go on and on until I can't stand any more and go to bed. I fall asleep, dreaming that Grand-mère lies in a coffin. It looks just like the iron lung that once kept me alive. Her head, adorned with a crown of red velvet ribbons, sticks out from the spongy collar at one end. Above her head is the little mirror angled to let her see people behind her. She sees me – or is it my mother? – and scowls, "Tisk, tisk."

I wake up, finding it hard to breathe. The memory of the iron lung presses heavily upon me. I dress quickly. I feel an urgent need to make my mother take me to Montréal. Grand-mère wants us all together. We are a family.

But she's gone.

My father sits alone in the kitchen, stirring a cup of coffee, and I collapse into a chair beside him.

He senses my question before I even ask. "She took the early train to Montréal." He taps his spoon against the cup. "She thought it best to go alone."

"I … she …" I push my breakfast dishes away and fold my elbows across the table, comforting my head in the cradle of my arms. "I wanted to say goodbye to Grand-mère. I wanted to see Tante Marie."

I feel my father's hand stroking my back. "Your mother's grieving."

"So am I!"

"I know. I wish she'd let you go, but she asked for some time alone. Losing her mother – I guess it's like the last door to her past, to Québec, closing. She can never go back home. She's had to say goodbye to so much."

But I'm not listening anymore. Say goodbye? What does she know about saying goodbye? What did she ever lose? Did she ever lose her best friend? Everything that counted in her world? She's mean, that's all, keeping me from Grand-mère's funeral, keeping me from Tante Marie. She's selfish. Well, I can be too.

I lift up my head and stare so intently at my father that he stops talking.

"What?"

"She's not here. She can't stop us if she's not here. She can't worry."

He stares back. Understanding lights his eyes.

"I've waited all winter. It was my gift. She didn't mind when we went to the Leafs game, remember?"

"What do you mean, she didn't mind? She was waiting up for us, pacing at the door!"

"Dad. Going to that game was the best thing that's happened to me in four years."

For the last week, since going to Maple Leaf Gardens, I've replayed the game over and over on my window seat rink. I feel again the cold air of the Gardens making me shiver, and I hear the thunder of the roaring crowds as the Leafs score the winning goal against the Canadiens. I stand to cheer wildly for my idols, just like everybody else.

Dad does this funny up-and-down Groucho Marx thing with his bushy eyebrows when his mind switches gears or when he's thinking something he's not going to say. "Hmm. It's tempting, very tempting."

"Please, Dad. My one dream in life is to play hockey."

"Ah well. I guess we didn't promise your mother, did we."

I have to press my advantage. I stand up and move as fast as I can to the door. "I'll bundle up. Meet you at the side door."

In less than five minutes we're out on the rink. Dad tucks the blanket around my legs in the wheelchair and passes me a shovel.

"Zamboni!" I whoop.

Dad laughs and starts to push me in the chair. We clear circles around the rink, pausing every few feet so I can throw loads of snow along the sides.

"Ready!" I puff when the rink is clear.

He hands me my stick, then starts to skate behind me slowly.

"I'll throw out the puck. See if you can pick it up and keep it on your stick."

A black puck comes skittering to a stop about twenty feet in front of me. I lean forward and capture it against the blade of my stick as we go by.

"Ha! Got ya!"

We approach the goal and I flick the puck as hard

as I can. It flies past the left post and bounces off the fence behind the net.

"Good try! Hold on!" Dad roars as we go behind the net, turning hard. Automatically, I lean the other way to keep from falling out of the chair.

We round the curve and I just manage to pick up the puck.

"Well done, Paulie."

Back and forth and around we go, twenty or thirty times. Each time I get better with the stick, and soon I rarely lose the puck when we turn a corner. Dad stops in front of the net to give me a long lesson on how to shoot, how to raise the puck.

"Okay, Dad. Enough. I got it. Let's skate again." How I love the ice flowing beneath my chair – *speed*. The air is cold, but I play a little game in my head, pretending I'm in Maple Leaf Gardens. I'm in the clear and the crowd is going wild.

"Faster!" I yell, and the chair soars down the ice as Dad digs in his edges.

Oh, we're moving now.

"Faster!"

We're starting to fly. My job is to raise the puck as we approach the net at full speed, seeking the sweet target of a corner pocket.

"She shoots, she scores!" Dad yells, and I smack Tante Marie's gift triumphantly against the ice.

On our last flight around the ice, he dumps me.

We hit a bump and I fly right out of the chair, sliding across the ice until I tangle to a stop in the bottom of the net. I roll over and sit up slowly. My bum is a bit sore, but that's all. I'm okay.

Dad rushes beside me, throwing up a spray of fine ice, falling to his knees.

"I'm not hurt, Dad." I smile at him. He collapses, half-hugging me, starting to laugh himself.

"She shoots, she scores!" he shouts again.

Suddenly, out of habit, we both look at the house, half-expecting to see my mother's anxious, disapproving face. But of course, she's not there. The windows are empty.

Wait – my dad's waving at someone, clapping his hands and cheering.

I follow his look. He's looking at Henry's house. At one of the windows I see Henry watching us. He's clapping and waving and has a happy grin on his face.

Dad and Henry are cheering for *me*.

Henry stops when he sees me staring at him.

Henry.

Now's my cue. He expects me to jerk my thumb at him and tell him where to go like I have for the last few years.

It all started when he gave me his sheriff's badge. He didn't understand what happened, how my thumb jerked as it came back to life. I didn't mean for him to go away. And then – it seemed too hard to change direction. Like sliding across the ice, it was impossible to stop.

I'm not mad at Henry anymore. I don't want to be mad at anyone. I want it to stop now.

I pick up my stick, lift it over my head and wave it at him.

He waves back.

It feels nice, *real* nice.

10.

TWO SESSIONS A DAY, 1955

Nurse Fredericks had a stern face and bluntly cut, steel-gray hair she stabbed off her face with steel bobby-pins that probably grew in her hair.

"You're the elective mute, are you?" she said. Even her voice matched her hair. Nothing soft or fanciful about it.

"You're going to get the Sister Kenny treatments. Hot packs, followed by stretching. You can't stretch your muscles, so I'm going to stretch them for you."

She picked up a steaming towel from a hot water bath beside my bed.

"Good thing you're dumb. I don't stand for screamers."

And she wrapped the near-scalding towel around my leg. I bit my lips to keep the scream in.

"Hmmph," she said, looking at my face. "It's got to be hot to do any good. Sister Kenny says so."

I didn't know who Sister Kenny was. But I hated her.

Gradually though, as the towel cooled, the heat felt good. Why, I wondered, couldn't Nurse Fredericks have waited a minute until the towel felt this good?

After the hot packs, there was worse. Nurse Fredericks lifted my leg into the air and held it, pushing it as far as it would go. I had never known such pain. Every feeling nerve inside me was screaming to run away.

Unbelievably she pushed harder. And held it again.

I couldn't keep it in. I moaned. Tears rushed down my face though there was no one to wipe them. *Mom! Dad!* I cried silently. *Please come save me!*

Nurse Fredericks seemed pleased. "That's it. No complaining now. We've got to stretch those lazy muscles. They've been lying around all these months, and I'll be helping you every day to get them back to work."

Mom! Dad! They had to come get me out of here. I'd have to tell them. I'd have to talk. But what if they didn't believe me? I wished Tante Marie would come. She always sat eye-level when she talked to me and listened intently to everything I said. She'd believe me. If only she could visit me. But she was far away in Paris and didn't know what was happening here.

Nurse Fredericks worked on all my muscles, and just when I thought I was going to die, she stopped. I lay panting, moaning inwardly as she wheeled me back to the ward.

"I'll see you later this afternoon," she said. "You'll be getting your physio twice a day."

Mom! Dad! Two sessions every day? How would I stand it?

Back in the ward, Bernardo whispered to me, "You're alive! How'd you like the torture?"

I laughed so hard, I began to cry. Big, huge sobs I could finally let out without fear of Nurse Fredericks hurting me worse. Or Witch Wilson hearing me.

They were all silent in their cribs, watching me, waiting for my crying to stop.

My nose ran and I desperately needed to blow it. But I couldn't move my hand, even to wipe my nose. So I lay there and turned my head as far as I could, trying to rub the slobber off my face into my pillow.

I looked at Bernardo. My eyes must have held so many questions.

"Your legs are still red," he said. "She makes the packs too hot. I heard it's not the way Sister Kenny wants. But that's Nurse Fredericks for you."

He must have felt sorry for me. "If she likes you, she'll start to make them less hot," he added kindly. "My dad explained to me why those exercises are important; they keep the muscles stretched. Otherwise your feet might drop straight down or your legs bend backward. You don't want that, right?"

I shook my head. But how would I stand it? Every morning. Every afternoon. Two sessions a day.

Torture.

Please God, I prayed. I'll be good. I won't complain. I won't scream.

Just get me out of here. Just get me home.

II.

SECOND CHANCE SPRING, 1960

When my mother gets back from the funeral in Montréal, she watches Dad and me play hockey. She paces back and forth at the side as Dad pushes me slowly around the rink. We don't dare go full speed.

I show her the slap shot I'm learning.

"Don't lean so far forward. You might fall out," she cries. "Are your arms strong enough for that? What if you crash into the boards?"

"Enough!"

"Relax, Agatha," Dad calls. "Isn't she great?"

Amazingly, she nods back. "Yes. Yes. She is great."

She turns away though, and goes inside. I stare at Dad. "What was that all about?"

"She's trying to relax a bit. Let you go. She had

some talks with her sisters. Sisters are good for that, or so I'm told."

She can relax all she likes; I'm not convinced she'll ever change.

I suggest to Dad that we skate every Saturday morning. That's my mother's morning for shopping and taking out half the books from the Don Mills library. We can fly around the rink unobserved.

The very next Saturday morning my mother goes out as usual, but someone else is watching. Henry leans over the fence and watches us skate around the rink until we come close to where he's standing.

"Need a goalie?" he asks. "I could dig the pucks out of the net or get the ones that go over the fence. You'd get more playing time."

Dad doesn't answer. There's a huge silence.

"**Yes!**" It comes out too loud and echoes across the rink. Oh great. The whole neighborhood has heard me finally speak to Henry.

Henry smiles. Then he nods, first at me, then at my Dad. "Okay, Paulie. Great. I'll be right over."

• • •

Henry plays with us every Saturday morning until the end of March. All too soon, it's spring and the snow and the rink are gone.

Henry suggests putting the nets on the road so we

can play road hockey together.

"On the street?" my mother says. "I think that's far too dangerous."

Henry glances at me. I don't know what to say. I'd like to. Inside I'm glowing, just glowing because he asked. But I don't want to tell him – at least not in front of my mother – how afraid I am of people gawking at me when they walk or drive by. I might as well be on TV.

"How about the driveway, then," Henry suggests. "That's safe."

Dad, Henry and my mother all turn to stare at me.

"I don't know, Henry. I'll have to think about it."

Henry looks disappointed. Some time I'll have to explain how much I hate when kids call me Polio-Pauline or Frankenstein, or when they imitate the way I walk.

My dad knows what I'm thinking about. After dinner it's still light out and he says, "How about a little walk?" Through the open window we can hear kids playing tag on the street. "Work up your strength," he adds, but I know he really means my courage.

That first walk through kids playing, I stare at the pavement. I'm sure I can hear heads turning as I lurch down the driveway. My dad is calling out "Hello" to neighbors, but thankfully he doesn't stop to talk. My ears feel ten times bigger than usual from the strain of listening to what the kids are saying. I'm sure I catch "There's Pauline," but nothing more. They keep right on playing their game. Screams of "You're it!" grow fainter behind us, and as they fade away, so does some of my fear.

I have survived. I have not died of embarrassment. Next time I vow to hold my head up and look them in the eye.

After that we go for a walk every evening. I suggest we walk farther and longer, twice around the block, and hey, how about trying new streets. This spring, I don't want to stay inside. Every day I feel stronger and I like it. I'm drawn to the front window, watching and wondering who the kids are that I see walking down the street, where they're going … and would they slow down a bit if I were with them?

Two long rainy weekends round out April, and Henry comes over during both. We play table hockey on my window seat. He wins every game. I teach him a few poker games and win a few of his comic books. We laugh a lot.

May. The evenings are warm and long and I ask Dad if we can walk all the way to the park to sit on the swings, staying out with the light. Sometimes my mother comes too, but she always bugs me about the books she has piled beside my window seat. I still pretend I haven't read them.

"*Heidi*'s a classic, Pauline. And *The Secret Garden*. I want to discuss them with you."

"If you'd let me go to school, I could discuss books there."

"Go to school?"

She's shocked. Her mouth is a perfect O, the same shape as the round, tight bun at the back of her head.

Her voice wobbles. "If they allow you to go … do you think you could manage?"

"B goes to school and he's doing fine. I'll never know if I don't try. I bet at school I wouldn't have to read books about crippled people."

I've gone too far. I see tears starting in her eyes.

My mother turns and walks away quickly.

Dad and I are left alone on the swings. The only sound is the *creak, creak* of the rusty chain.

Dad leans back and looks at the sky for what seems forever, then sits up.

"I forget what happens in *Heidi*. Tell me."

"She befriends a girl in a wheelchair. She gets up and walks at the end too, just like Colin does in *The Secret Garden*."

Dad swings for a minute, pumping high, then jumps off and turns around to face me.

"Your mother loves books. There's got to be something good about *Heidi*. Sometimes we need to give books, just like people, a second chance."

Strange, how Dad finds the sharpest words to needle under my skin, words like *giving people a second chance*. I hang my head. I've been wishing lately that I could have a best friend to be with. Sure I'm still friends with B, but that's only through letters and because we survived polio together. Now I want real, ordinary friends in my life, like Mary Lennox or Heidi ... or Henry.

Dad's probably not thinking about friends. He means my mother. Why don't I give my mother a second chance? Is it because I got polio? Because I can't walk perfectly? Because she didn't protect me back then when I needed it?

Dad moves forward and holds onto the chains on either side of me, holding the swing steady. He lifts my chin so I have to look him in the eye.

Something starts to tumble around inside me. Dad's good at seeing both sides of a problem. I throw myself against him and hide my face in the clean sky-blue of his cotton shirt.

"The thing is ..." I cry, "I still want that happy ending. The running and skating one."

He rubs my back. "Aw, Paulie," he says softly. "You'll have a happy ending. It just might look a little different."

I look up at him and wipe my runny nose across my elbow.

"Very nice. You've soaked my shirt," he laughs, handing me one of his white handkerchiefs. "Let's go home. It's still early."

"Okay. Yeah. I'm ready."

As we round the corner onto Chelsea, I see Henry out in his driveway with his hockey net, shooting balls, drinking a Coke. Wouldn't it be a great second chance to play out on the street again with Henry? How would I manage it? With my crutches? Impossible. And what about having half of Don Mills watching? But what's the worst that can happen? Everybody's seen me lurch up and down the street for weeks now. If anybody stares, I can outstare them.

My heart's racing as we get closer and closer to his driveway. He's turning around.

"Hi, Henry. Need a goalie?" I ask.

"Hey, Pauline. That'd be great."

Dad's eyebrows are doing their Groucho Marx thing. He walks away saying, "I'll go get your wheel-chair. You'll need it for goal."

Dad knows I don't like being in a wheelchair if I can help it. Wheelchairs tell the whole world you can't walk. But I remind myself that a wheelchair let me play hockey on our backyard rink. And maybe now I'll play hockey on the street.

Henry's whacking his stick across the asphalt. "There's a new shot I'm learning. It's called a slap shot."

"Okay," I say.

He turns and shoots a ball into the net. He shoots hard. Suddenly I wonder if I can stop his shot. Will it hurt if it hits me?

"I haven't played much goal."

"Don't worry. I won't give you my hardest shot." He fishes in a can of equipment beside the garage. "I've got goalie gloves."

Dad's back with my old wheelchair. He wheels me into the net and Henry tosses me the gloves. They're made for giants. I stick a giant leather hand out as if a ball is coming to the right of me. Open and close.

Dad's grinning like crazy. "I have a phone call to make. Keep the brakes on, Paulie, or your mother will give me heck. Have fun."

My mind's in a whirl. I'm playing on the street for the first time in years … goalie for Henry … I hate wheelchairs … but I'm out!

Henry doesn't give me time to dwell on anything. He shoots the ball fast, down on the right. Automatically I reach … and miss. I groan. I want to be good at this. The ball rolls out of the net and I whack it angrily back to Henry.

"I've got five balls here," he says. "I'll shoot 'em one after the other. Send 'em all back together."

I nod. Geez – I know what to do! Haven't I watched years of road hockey from a window? I lean over, right arm extended. Even if I have to throw myself out of this wheelchair, I'll stop one of the next five balls. I'll show Henry.

Henry shoots the balls fast, one after the other, always down on the right.

I catch the last one.

"Ha!" I gloat, holding it high in the air. "You're going to have to shoot harder than that."

Henry smiles at me. "You haven't changed, Paulie."

"What do you mean by that?"

He lines up the five balls again, getting ready to shoot. "Just that you're fun to play with."

His words make me tingle with pleasure. But his next ball whips right at my head and I block it with my glove, just in time.

"Hey, are you trying to kill me?"

Henry's mouth drops open and his forehead bunches up with worry.

Me and my stupid mouth. I've scared him. "I didn't mean that. Don't worry. I'll be ready for it this time."

But he pauses, looking less sure of what he's doing. "I can't guarantee I won't hit you."

"I'll pay you back somehow. Don't worry about it."

He rests his square chin on his hands, clasping the end of his stick, and says softly, "I had enough paybacks, don't you think?"

I feel the blood gush into my face. He's not talking about the ball. He means the *Go away*, and me not talking to him for so long. Tears well at the back of my eyes, but no way will I let myself cry.

Darn this boy anyway! What does he know about anything?

He walks halfway toward me. "Do you remember those horses your dad made us? I had the blue one. You had the red one."

Do I remember? How could I forget? I nod.

"Do you remember … I let you take the lead that day?" He pauses awkwardly. "It was your birthday. For a long, long time I thought it was my fault you got polio. Because I let you take the lead."

I stare at him, uncomprehending. How could he think anything so stupid?

"My dad always taught me that boys should take care of girls. Hold the door and all that stuff. And we were chasing bad guys, remember?"

I suddenly realize what Henry's about to say next.

"I blamed myself. I should have been in the lead. Then I would have been the one to get polio, not you. I let the bad guys get you, Paulie."

"That's not how a virus works …"

He interrupts me. "I *know* the scientific explanation. We studied all about Salk's vaccine in school, believe me. But …" he brushes his light brown hair back from his forehead as if it will clear his thoughts. "It's the darndest thing. When you got polio, I believed it was all my fault."

Imagine that. Henry thought it was his fault. Neither of us understood what was happening. Nobody talked about it or explained it to us.

I dig the ball out of the net where it's stuck in the webbing, freeing it. There's so much to talk about; maybe I can do it too. Yet somehow it's harder to talk face-to-face with a friend than it is to write it down in a letter.

"You want to know what I believed?" I ask shyly, checking Henry's face first. He nods seriously, listening.

"I thought it was because I had the red horse. Remember when my dad made them, and we both wanted the red horse? I pouted and you let me have my way. I thought I was getting punished for being so selfish."

"Gee." Henry lets out a long breath. "Guess we were both dumb."

"My dad had to burn those horses. The hospital told him they were contaminated."

All of a sudden he asks me, "Why wouldn't you speak to me?"

I get that ornery, prickly feeling all over me again – the one that gets me into so much trouble. "How would *you* like not being able to skate or run?" I say before I can stop myself.

"I wouldn't."

"Even if it's a virus … it could have been you, just as easily."

"I know that."

But he's mad, I can hear it in his voice. He turns away and walks back to the balls, lined up, waiting.

How'd we get into this?

Henry shoots a ball, really hard. It zings by my left shoulder, and stupidly I watch it stick in the netting.

"Good shot," I whisper.

"I need a goalie. Are you going to try or not?"

I breathe deep, lean forward and stick both gloves out.

"Left side. Get ready." He shoots the remaining four and I miss them all.

"I'm no good on the left side."

"Then I'll keep shooting them there. It's the only way to get better."

We play for a while, but it's starting to get dark.

"I can't see the ball coming."

"Let's stop." He shoves all the equipment in the big can, and the net at the side of the garage, harder than he needs to. "Your dad's having a long phone call. Shall I take you home?"

I nearly say, *I can walk by myself.* But I think better of it. It's all over Henry's face that he's struggling with something. So instead, I say, "He's probably got my mother stuffed in a closet so she can't come out here and watch us."

Henry doesn't say anything.

"She doesn't want me to go to school. Thinks I'll be sick all the time and worn out. She thinks kids will be cruel and say stuff. But you should see the awful stuff she makes me read. Classics."

"Mothers are all the same. You should hear my mother yell when Lisa and I read comics all day. She yells we're reading garbage."

"I've heard. You only live next door."

Finally he smiles a little. "Maybe you should try Nancy Drew. My mom doesn't seem to mind those books and Lisa's crazy about them."

"What are they about?"

"Some girl detective."

"Sounds good."

"I'll lend you one."

We're at my front door already. Henry passes me my crutches and puts the wheelchair in the garage.

In the last light of the summer evening, silence stretches between us like a long, winter shadow. There's so much more to talk about, but it's stuck, frozen in this silence between us. How do we become friends again? What would he do if I told him about the House of Horrors? About Witch Wilson? About really being stuffed in a closet?

"Thanks, Henry. Maybe next time you'll let me shoot."

Henry doesn't smile. He nods goodnight and turns away to go home. Just like that. I lean after him, hungry for more, wishing he'd stay and talk.

But tonight, it's his turn not to speak.

12.

NURSE NIGHTINGALE, 1955

I have a few wonderful memories from the six months I spent in the House of Horrors.

B. He was everybody's best friend. Mine too.

He turned Witch Wilson and Nurse Fredericks into a game, thinking up new ways to get back at them. B had the gift of mimicry and as soon as Witch Wilson left the ward, he'd stand up in his crib and imitate her, making us laugh so hard we had to be careful not to wet our beds.

My parents came to see me every Sunday – the only time we were allowed visitors. It had been five months since my father had carried me out of my house to the car to take me to the hospital. Five months … it felt like forever.

And then Nurse Nightingale appeared. She was

something wonderful too. One Saturday afternoon when she was working, instead of taking her break she asked if I would like to look out the window.

My eyes must have popped the question, *How*? I could wiggle toes and fingers and turn my neck. That was it.

She held out her arms. "Trust me? I'll carry you."

She picked me up and I relaxed against her chest. I could feel a bit of starch in her white dress – it was clean and reassuring, like the smell of soap about her. She was humming something under her breath that sounded like "Somewhere over the Rainbow" from *The Wizard of Oz*. I'd seen it twice. It was my favorite movie, my favorite song.

I smiled and hummed along in my mind.

She rested my bottom against the windowsill, never letting go of me. Her arms were as strong as any chair. I couldn't sit up or move, but if I could have, I would have wrapped my arms around her neck.

I think that's where my love of sitting at a window started. It was the first time in five months I had felt safe and ordinary, like once-upon-a-time. I was me again, if only for a few minutes.

It was winter outside. The sun sparkled in the snow, and I could tell by the crisp blue sky that it was a very cold day. The birch tree beside the long drive-way was bare of leaves, and a blue jay perched in one of the top branches. It surprised me, so intensely blue against the white bark. And still here in winter, just like me, still here.

I felt happy to be alive, perched in the warm circle of Nurse Nightingale's white, uniformed arms.

I blew a foggy circle on the window and, with my nose, drew a happy face.

Nurse Nightingale kissed my forehead. "Thank you, Pauline. I'm so glad it makes you happy."

She never once tried to make me speak.

I think maybe she was an angel.

13.

GOOD NEWS, 1960

Over the summer, my shot gets pretty good. But I'm frustrated with the arms of the wheelchair. "They're in my way!" I say, pounding them with a fist. My dad argues that they provide something to hold onto, along with extra protection.

"Off!" I appeal to Henry. He sees the problem. Henry looks at Dad, and next thing I know, the armrests are gone. Suddenly I'm free to lean out as far as I dare and get the full power of my shoulders into the swing.

Stuart and Billy watch us the way Henry did in the beginning, and before I can say *August*, they're playing too. We have a regular Saturday morning game. For my thirteenth birthday, we play road hockey on the street and then come inside for card games and chocolate cake.

It's the best birthday party in a long time.

Then school starts again. I find the weekdays at home too long. I easily finish the work my mother assigns me. By three o'clock I watch at the front kitchen window for the kids to come home from school.

"I want to go to school like everybody else," I tell my mother. She's sitting at the kitchen table, checking my map of Europe. The bun of her hair sits like a lonely mountain peak at the back of her head. She takes off her reading glasses and stares at me, her fingers smoothing the already smooth map.

Outside, kids are yelling things at each other as they pass by, coming home.

She surprises me. "Okay. I'll phone the principal of Don Mills Junior High," she says slowly. "We can arrange a visit and see what you think."

There's a catch. "In return, I want you to re-read *Heidi* and *The Secret Garden* … all the books piled up beside your window seat. I think we need to discuss them."

I pretend a reluctant agreement. Secretly I've read all the books, *Heidi* and *The Secret Garden* three times. Each time I like Heidi and Mary Lennox more and more. They're now my secret friends; will I meet girls like them at school? I cried reading about Roosevelt in the book about U.S. presidents. Finally, a cripple who doesn't walk at the end! He had a dream and followed it right into the White House. It makes me wonder if my mother understands that I have dreams too. Yet when the time comes to talk with her, I can't help but fight.

"Well, did you learn anything from these books?" she asks me.

"When are we visiting the school?"

"Tuesday. But first, we discuss the book about the U.S. presidents."

My feelings go up and down like a teeter-totter when I talk with my mother. "You want me to say how inspired I am that Franklin Roosevelt had polio and was a great president of the United States. Right? Well …"

She's smiling, looking pleased at my words. Why can't I stay positive? I *was* inspired by Roosevelt. But the teeter-totter is going down. I feel all prickly and ornery, ready for a fight.

"But they never took his picture once in a wheel-chair or with crutches. Even his statue doesn't show him the way he really was. He had to pretend he had no trouble walking. Why? Wouldn't people vote for a cripple?"

For once, my mother doesn't try to talk me out of my feelings. "He did hide some of his struggle. But …" she struggles to find the right words, "it was a time when attitudes were less accepting. People were so terrified of polio. And remember, being the president of the United States was a grave responsibility. It was the depression, then the war. More than ever, people needed to believe in their leader."

"If they can't let the president have polio, who will ever believe in me?"

"Your dad does, and …" she smoothes the map one more time, "I do."

I feel as if someone's jumped off the other end of the teeter-totter and I've crashed to the ground. *Whomp.*

"You do not! You don't really want me to go to school. You worry about every little thing I do. You'd be happy if I never went outside this house."

She winces. She stops smoothing the paper and squeezes both hands tightly together. "Maybe you're right. Your father says the same thing. So did Grand-mère. But," she says, lifting her chin, "it's not because I don't believe in you."

"Oh yeah. What is it?"

"I don't believe in the world out there. I won't trust an institution again."

I remember the House of Horrors. "I'm growing up. I can handle things. I want to try."

"I know. I know. But you don't have to throw yourself out there recklessly. That's Marie's way, and it's not a good one. Better to take small, careful steps. You're outside more, playing hockey. Isn't that enough for now?"

I'm back on the teeter-totter, mad at her again.

Why does she have to criticize Tante Marie?

"I just want to go to school!"

She throws up her hands, exasperated. "I'm *trying*, Pauline! We'll go for a visit on Tuesday. You'll see for yourself. It's not going to be so easy."

She's right, too. We visit the school the following week. It is not what I'd hoped for. There are obvious problems and it's confusing.

Half the classes are upstairs. Mr. Dunlop, the principal, smiles at me nervously and assures me that he understands how courageous I must be to want to come to school. He wishes he could help, but, he hums and haws, he can't arrange all my classes to be on the main floor. He stares at my brace. The science and language labs are all upstairs. Those classes are compulsory.

"Let's look at the stairs," my mother suggests. I can tell she's annoyed at him.

We go out in the hallway to look at the stairs. There's a lot of them. Stairs are hard for me. Exhausting! The metal brace supporting my left leg comes up to my thigh and I can't bend my knee. Can I do it? Can I?

There's only one way to know.

"I'll try the stairs. Can you time me?"

"Oh, I don't know if you should do this," the principal starts.

But my mother cuts him off. Her face is drained of color and she looks upset, but she stares down the principal. "She asked us to time her. Ready?"

I don't do stairs the way Nurse Fredericks taught me, using the support of both crutches. I made up my own way. I put both crutches under my left arm, lean heavily on the banister on my right side, swing my left leg out and up as I balance on my good leg. My mother is strangely quiet beside me, never saying a word.

I gaze up the stairs. It's a long way. The school is quiet. Behind me, behind the closed doors, in the classrooms are the other kids. Working. I want to be here too.

I do one stair at a time. There are twelve to the landing and then another set of twelve. When I'm almost at the top, a teacher comes down the hallway, carrying papers. He reminds me of the principal. He wears a dark jacket over a white shirt and tie, and he doesn't look happy to see me.

"Ahh … do you need help?"

"No," I tell him. "Thank you," remembering to be polite. I guess he's never seen anyone in crutches on these stairs.

I swing my left leg up the last stair, turn around and prepare to go down. The teacher's behind me. I can feel his fear following me.

I go back down the stairs. This time the crutches go down first.

I'm breathing hard when I reach the bottom.

"Ten minutes," the principal says, dismayed.

"You did it!" my mother says. I hear pride in her voice.

I lean against the wall. I can imagine what the principal and the teacher are thinking. Five minutes up. Five minutes down. I'll be late for every class. And what if someone jostles me down the stairs?

Then a bell rings, loud in my ears, and I jump. All of a sudden, doors along the hallway bang open and kids pour out from all directions. Everybody is carrying books. How will I manage these crowds with my crutches? Kids see me and walk past as if I'm invisible. But I see them peek back, staring at me resting heavily on my crutches. No one smiles. No one comes close.

Suddenly I see Stuart O'Connor, his freckled face and curly hair. He sees me and waves, runs toward me with a big, friendly smile. I feel like crying as he approaches.

"Hey, Pauline! Whatcha doing?"

"Hi, Stu. Checking out the school."

The boy beside him shuffles from one foot to the other, gawking at me, then looking away down the hall. I bet he's never seen a leg like mine before.

"Maybe I can give you a tour."

"Come on, Stu," the other boy says uneasily. "We're going to be late for math."

"I'd rather take Pauline on a tour," Stu says, laughing at his obvious ploy to miss class. Another bell rings and the other boy pulls his sleeve, heading down the hallway.

"Guess I better go. You should check out the gym, Pauline. Show Miss McCarthy your shot. See ya Saturday."

We don't do a tour. I'm anxious to go home. There are too many problems to sort out and my head is spinning. My mother asks me what I think and I tell her I don't know. I put school in the back closet of my mind with a sign on it: Undecided. It's not just the stairs. It's those kids staring at me, keeping their distance. Could I stand it?

Here on my window seat it's lonely, but no one's afraid of me.

• • •

Saturday morning, as usual, Henry, Stuart and Billy call on me for a game of road hockey. My mother's okay about it, as long as Dad plays too. She can't help worrying about the road. The boys like my dad with us. So do I. With Dad pushing me, I can play forward. We're getting fast – and good.

But the last Saturday in October, just before we get ready to go out, my mother stops me.

"Before you go out, there's something we've been meaning to tell you."

Dad buttons up his coat, looking uncomfortable. "Do you think this is the moment?"

The way they're looking at each other, I know it's

something big. "What's the matter? Did someone die?"

"No," my father laughs at me. "The opposite. Your mother is going to …"

I gasp, feeling stupid, noticing for the first time the slight bulge of her usually flat belly. Suddenly I realize she has been wearing loose-fitting dresses for a while instead of skirts. My mother's pregnant! How awful!

"How could you?" I blurt out, feeling betrayed. Aren't I good enough? "You're too old."

"I am not!" she cries, indignant.

"We don't need a baby."

"We're having one."

"Maybe it will get polio."

I hear her sharp intake of breath. "Pauline … how can you say that? That's so cruel."

I shove my toque down over my ears. It's simple: I don't want a sister or brother who can run or skate. Especially not now, not when things are starting to turn around for me.

My father puts an arm around each of us, but I shrug him off and glare at the black-and-white linoleum floor.

"There's the vaccine now," he says. "Thank God, it won't happen again. This baby will be a blessing for all of us."

"When's the *blessing* coming?" I ask sarcastically.

My mother is leaning against my father, his arms

wrapped protectively around her. "If you mean the baby," she says, "it's due in March. Your father will be allowed in the hospital and will spend a lot of time there. But you won't be allowed in. Someone will have to stay at home with you." She hesitates. "I've asked my sisters."

My throat aches with hope. After being so mean, do I dare ask? "Tante Marie?"

"You'd like that, wouldn't you?" Her hand skates uneasy circles around her belly.

Why should I have to have a sibling? I can hear in my mother's voice how much she hates her own sister. I feel like I'm about to explode. I have to get outside. I'm not going to beg anything from my mother, not even a visit from Tante Marie.

I open the door and shuffle outside. Dad makes a move behind me, but I yell over my shoulder, "I can do this myself. I'll play goal today. I don't need you. Leave me alone."

I don't bother to turn around to see their reaction. They have each other.

I storm — carefully — out onto the street. Henry and Stuart and Billy have stopped in the middle of a play and are watching me approach. I get the uneasy feeling they heard me yelling.

"Where's your dad?" Billy asks.

I don't trust myself to talk. I jerk my thumb back in the direction of my house.

Henry looks like an owl, staring at me. "Get her chair, will ya, Stu? How about we put the nets at the curbs and play two on two? Pauline can play goal and she won't have to worry about cars."

I glare at him. Overprotective Henry. Of all the nerve. If I didn't have to hold onto my crutches, I'd jerk my thumb at him too.

Henry's wearing his Don Mills hockey jacket, blue with white piping around the shoulder seams. It's cold and his breath shows — white piping against the sky. Billy shoves his hands in his jeans pockets and now Stu's back, huffing and puffing with my chair.

What am I so mad at? Out of nowhere the tears start dribbling down my cheeks and I wipe my face on my sleeve.

The three boys move in a little closer and stand in a semi-circle around me.

"What's wrong, Pauline?" asks Henry.

"You don't have to play goal if you don't want," says Billy.

"We could go watch boxing on TV at my house," says Stu.

Henry hits Stu with his hat. "Idiot. She doesn't want to watch fighting."

I half-laugh, half-cry. These guys are funny. Are these guys my friends?

"My parents are going to have a baby," I confide.

It sounds so silly when I say it, but they all make a

big *Ooohhh* as if I've revealed something terrible. I remember that they each have younger kids in their families. Billy has two little brothers and a sister, and some Saturday mornings he can't play because he has to babysit.

"That's too bad," Stu says. "My little brother's a real nuisance. He's always switching the channel or talking or …"

Henry hits him again. "She doesn't need to hear that part. She needs to hear the good part."

"What's the good part?"

Henry runs his fingers through his hair. I know he fights with his sister. I hear them sometimes over the fence or through the windows in the summer.

"Family," Billy pipes up decisively. "Imagine Christmas dinner. It's best when it's noisy and everybody's trying to talk at the same time. Or when you come home to brag about something and you get a big, loud cheer from the whole family. The more, the merrier, I say."

"Someone to take your side against your parents when they're being unfair."

"By the time this kid is old enough to take my side, I won't be living at home anymore," I argue.

"Aw, they're cute when they're little," Stu says. "They've got itsy-bitsy fingers and itsy-bitsy toes."

Henry hits him again.

"Now what'd you hit me for?"

"I don't know. Your itsy-bitsy brain, I guess."

I'm laughing now, slapping one crutch against the road.

"Billy!" We hear Billy's mother calling him from their front door down the street.

Billy grabs his stick. "I gotta babysit. See? There's the bad part. That's tough news, Pauline. Real tough. You coming, Stu? Your brother's playing at our house today. I hate your brother more than you do. What a pest. Come on."

"I guess we'll watch cartoons." They're walking away, but we can hear them.

"No way. My mom hates cartoons. She says we can watch that garbage over her dead body. Can you imagine? You come home one Saturday and there's your mom, dead on the living room floor, and you jump right over her because the first thing you think is, oh great! Now I can watch cartoons. Does your mom say dumb stuff ..."

They laugh, hitting each other until I can't hear them clearly anymore. I look at Henry, but he's not smiling. He takes off his toque and twirls it around his index finger.

"So, do you like Lisa?" I ask him.

"She's a little sister. Little sisters can be very an-noying."

"So ... you don't."

"Look. You don't always like your brother or sister

or even your best friend every minute of every day. But they're good for all kinds of stuff. They're family." He pauses meaningfully. "Why'd you get so mad at your dad?" He kicks his foot against the curb. "You've got a temper. I worry some day that you'll stop talking to me again, just like that." He snaps his fingers.

I take a big breath and let it out. "Sometimes I get mad at the world. Don't you?"

How'd we get back to this? It must have something to do with what I said about not wanting the baby. Even though I don't quite get the connection, I blurt out, "You guys helped. I'm feeling better about having a brother or sister. Even if they can walk and run and skate …"

I stop and shake my head really hard, because I can't lie – I do not want a brother or sister who can skate. "Anyway, I'll try and be happy about it. Who knows, it might be good for all of us. My mother can worry and fuss over Itsy-Bitsy instead of me, right?"

Finally, Henry laughs. I laugh with him. Henry has this wide smile that goes a little lopsided sometimes. Like right now.

All afternoon, I don't mind playing goal for Henry. And as we laugh and yell, I play with a new thought. It's starting to feel okay.

I'm going to be a big sister.

14.

THE NEW BRACE AND
SHOE, 1955

Six months in the House of Horrors.

Physio with Nurse Fredericks twice a day. My muscles gradually came back, except the ones in my left leg. That leg stayed thin and small no matter how much Nurse Fredericks pushed and moved it. I wore a big, clumsy brace around it that I hated. But at the same time, the brace supported me as I learned to walk again.

The first time I walked, leaving my wheelchair, I could only manage a few steps on crutches. But I felt as if I'd run around the world. I thought I'd burst with happiness. I could move, almost like once-upon-a-time, without a wheelchair.

Late in June I got a letter from Tante Marie. Her studies in Paris were almost over. She'd be coming home soon, but she wasn't going to fly to Montréal. She was coming to Toronto to see me first. Immediately. Me. I was important.

I kept Tante Marie's letter in the pocket of my shirt. I was so scared Witch Wilson would take it if she found it.

I worked very hard, walking every minute I could on my crutches. I was determined to be normal again. "You have to build up the muscle in your right leg to compensate for your left leg," Nurse Fredericks said, pushing, always pushing till I wanted to scream.

"You have to keep working hard for the next few years. Your right leg's coming along fine. I've ordered a new brace for your left leg, and shoes. They're special. They'll fit you much better. You'll be walking every day in them."

I was determined to walk, all right. Walk out of here and never come back.

My parents visited every Sunday but I still didn't speak. My mother held me in her arms, circling my arms, then my left leg, with her thumb and forefinger. "So thin. So thin, Pauline. You have to eat more."

She read to me too – all her favorites. Dad brought his little metal hockey players and we played a thousand games: Leafs against the Canadiens.

They brought me Orange Crush every visit and I gulped it greedily, without stopping. Witch Wilson would never take one from me again.

At night I had to sleep with metal braces strapped to both legs. My feet were locked into the braces to keep them from dropping. I hated the braces because I couldn't turn over in them, but I didn't drop-foot, whatever that was. My muscles were coming back to life, as if from a long sleep, but the braces knocked against the bars of my crib as I tossed and turned at night.

Nurse Fredericks had a final torture in store for me. One day she looked terribly pleased and clapped her hands as I entered. "Your new shoes and walking brace are here."

There on the floor were the ugliest shoes I'd ever seen. They were heavy, dark brown oxfords. It was silly, but I'd been dreaming that, just like Dorothy in *The Wizard of Oz*, I'd get dazzling, ruby red slippers to take me home.

Something in me rebelled. No! I wasn't going to wear those ugly oxfords. I wanted pretty shoes.

I glared at her and thrust out my jaw.

"You don't like them? We'll see about that."

She took my crutches. I teetered precariously. She forced me to sit down. I crossed my arms over my chest defiantly and she scolded me.

"You're lucky to get these shoes. Lucky to walk. Lucky to be alive. Now stop this nonsense." She grabbed my feet and pushed them into the stiff shoes, lacing them up so tight I couldn't bear it. Then she buckled the strap around the brace, again pulling too hard. It hurt.

I pushed her away and she toppled over, caught off guard.

Her face twisted with anger. She stood up and held up her hand as if to slap me. But she didn't.

"You naughty child!" she said. At that moment I hated Nurse Fredericks almost as much as Witch Wilson. Who was she to make me topple from "lucky" to "naughty" at her whim? She was a naughty nurse!

It wasn't over.

Roughly she handed me my crutches. A big metal knob pressed against the inside of my leg where the metal bar of the brace fit into the shoe. It rubbed against my ankle.

"Now walk," she ordered, handing me my crutches.

It was misery. They hurt. They were so tight and heavy that I could barely drag my left foot.

"Lift it up," she ordered sternly.

But every time I swung my left foot forward, the big metal knob bashed against my right ankle.

She made me walk back and forth, back and forth. Twenty times. The sock on my right ankle was red with blood.

I hated my new shoes and brace. But I hated her more.

All right, I vowed silently, knowing I only had one hope. I wouldn't give up. I'd wear the ugly shoes and heavy brace and I'd swing my left leg so the metal knob didn't bash against my ankle.

Soon, soon, I'd walk out of here and go home.

15.

MARCH THAW, 1961

The issue of school stays in the closet, undecided, over the winter. I want to go. I think about it. B writes and tells me to try it. School's like spaghetti, he says. Everybody makes it and eats it a different way. Yet every time I imagine that stairway, that hallway, bursting with kids avoiding me, I can't bring myself to do it.

Dad and I make a rink again. Henry suggests we put up sideboards with an opening for my wheelchair. Stu and Billy bring plywood and scraps of lumber from their garages and before long we've built the Don Mills Gardens. Dad builds a little bench beside the opening where we can put our skates on, and we play hockey every Saturday and Sunday with Henry, Stu and Billy. It's the highlight of my week. Thankfully the weather stays cold enough to keep the rink frozen right until

March, right until the day of Tante Marie's arrival.

With the approach of the train from Québec, the mercury fires up the thermometer outside our back window, and my mother goes into instant labor. By the time my father brings Tante Marie home from Union Station, gloomy pools of water threaten our rink, and my mother's contractions come regularly.

I wait on my window seat, listening to the lilt of Tante Marie's voice. I ignore the commotion in the front hall as my father fetches forgotten items for my mother's hospital bag. They kiss me hurriedly and are gone.

At long last I am alone with Tante Marie. We laugh and hug and can't get caught up quickly enough.

"I didn't see you for Grand-mère's death. Now I see you for a birth!" She shakes her head, her hair swinging freely. "It's got to mean something, don't you agree?"

"It means she has to have more babies!" I laugh, not really wanting it to be true. I pull out B's letter and hand it to Tante Marie. "He's still nuts about you. He wants you to know he's playing the drums in the school band."

Tante Marie takes the letter and puts it in her pocket. "That boy will be the conductor one day. I'll read it later. First, I have a special gift for *you*."

Tante Marie drags an enormous bag to my window seat. With a magician's flourish, she pulls out smocked dresses and knitted sets of matching baby booties and sweaters. I laugh with delight when, from the very bottom, she pulls out a red beret and twirls it on one finger.

"You're a teenager. I thought you might want to ..." she gives it to me and waves her hand in the air, searching for the right expression, "... go wild." Her eyes tease. "Your maman's going to wonder at me, not bringing you a book or a pretty dress."

"I hate dresses. You know that. They only show my legs."

I try on the beret.

"Ooh-la-la," she says, standing beside me and tilting it way down over my forehead. "You want to look dangerous, remember? With that beautiful hair of yours, you are going to make some boy's heart beat a little faster."

Me? Could my thick brown hair be beautiful? What does Henry think about my hair? I feel a little flip-flop in my stomach ... does he even notice?

"Hey," she says, looking in the big cabinet. "Where's that table hockey game you used to play with?"

"Top shelf. Unless my mother's thrown it out. She never liked it."

She finds the game and pulls it down. "*C'est fantastique.* What do you say we have our own Stanley Cup finals this week? Leafs against the Canadiens."

She winks at me. "Guess who I'm gonna be?"

I laugh. My very own blessing is right here. The Good Witch of the East come to save me.

Kneeling at the other end of my window seat, Tante Marie smokes and curses all week as we abandon ourselves to our hockey match. It's Toronto against Montréal, English against the French.

In a hospital downtown, my mother gives birth to a baby girl. When Dad calls to give us the news, Tante Marie is thrilled for me. I have a sister. Briefly I wonder if a sister is better or worse than a brother. We're having so much fun that I put that baby sister out of my thoughts.

The evening my dad is expected to bring Mom and the baby home, Henry knocks at the door with a gift. I hear Tante Marie invite him in and I quickly find my new red beret and tilt it to one side, dangerously, just like Tante Marie showed me.

Henry comes into the back room, shuffling from one foot to the other. I feel him staring at my beret.

"It's going below freezing tonight," he says. "Should be good for the rink. I ... that is, Stu and Billy ... I wondered if you wanted to play a game tomorrow."

Tante Marie is standing behind him. She raises her eyebrows and smiles a silent question at me.

"That would be great, Henry. I'd like that." I'll kill her later, if she doesn't stop.

"I'll phone Stu and Billy then. We can play in the

morning. Maybe we could help with the baby," he finishes lamely.

He turns to leave and bumps into Tante Marie. "Sorry. See ya, Paulie."

Tante Marie lets him out and comes back, stands in the doorway. "Help with the baby?"

I take off my beret and throw it at her. "His mother probably made him say that. He's our next-door neighbor."

She catches the beret and comes to sit at her end of the window seat. "And a very handsome one," she says.

I roll my eyes.

"Okay, okay. No more teasing. It's time for the playoffs."

16.

FACE-OFF: THE HOUSE OF HORRORS, 1955

In a way, it was thanks to Cindy that I went home.

On the same day that I got my new walking brace and the ugliest shoes in the world, Cindy arrived at the House of Horrors. Janet had gone home the week before and there was space in our ward for another girl. Cindy was five but appeared no bigger than a baby, lying motionless in her crib.

She looked so sad. I wanted to tell her, "You'll start to move soon too." But polio was tricky – we never knew how long it would take, or how much permanent damage had been done. There was no way of knowing if Cindy would regain a hand, a leg … or just one toe. But one thing we knew: she'd have to work hard.

Of course, I still didn't speak.

Thank God, Bernardo did.

Cindy's first night with us, all of us in the ward listened to her lonely cries in the dark after the nurse turned our lights out. We were separated by our cribs. But listening to her, I felt as if it were *me* crying. All of us in the ward were Cindy — we were all one child, paralyzed and scared, struggling to go back to our lives, determined to go back to our real, ordinary selves.

"When you stop that crying, Cindy," B called out loudly, in order to be heard, "I'll tell you a story."

"Tell the one about Cinderella," Lorna said. "That's my favorite."

"Where they race around in wheelchairs," called Frank.

The crying stopped and we heard long sniffs.

B waited a minute and then began to tell the story. *As a little girl, Cinderella, whose friends called her Cindy, had polio and was forced to live in a hospital under the care of her wicked stepsisters.*

The night nurse walked down the hallway past the ward. B paused briefly. When lights were out we were supposed to be quiet and go right to sleep. Maybe the night nurse knew what we had to endure with the day shift, with Witch Wilson.

Maybe the nurse knew how much we missed our moms and dads and needed a story to get to sleep. We heard her footsteps get softer and softer, allowing

B to finish the story. *The prince had polio too and they raced around the ballroom in their wheelchairs. Together they chased the wicked stepsisters away and they were never allowed to bother children in hospitals again.*

The next morning, however, we knew there'd be a problem. There was a bad smell – and it came from Cindy's bed.

We could hear the breakfast trolley rumbling down the hallway. No one said a word.

Maybe, I hoped, Cindy will be lucky and there will be another nurse on duty, one of the nice ones.

But no. Witch Wilson stood in the doorway. She took three bowls of cereal off the trolley and thunked them on the little table where B, Mary and I now ate, unassisted. She let down the bars of our cribs and we were expected to make our own way over to the table to feed ourselves.

Then she must have smelled it, for she stopped in the middle of the ward, sniffing the air. Her eyes darted around the room, accusing each of us until they rested on the new girl, Cindy.

"What do I smell? Someone couldn't wait?"

She stalked over to Cindy's bed and put her hands on her hips. "You'll learn. Just like everyone else here. I don't put up with this nonsense. I have five of you to feed and change and get ready for the day. All by myself, you hear? I got no time to clean up a big girl like you who can't wait. So you're going to have to learn not to do this again. Do you understand?"

Cindy began to cry again. I felt like crying too. It was awful, having the nurse yell at you for something you couldn't help.

"None of that. I don't stand for crying."

Cindy cried loudly, "Mommy! I want my mommy!"

That did it. Witch Wilson took the crib brakes off and wheeled Cindy down to the far end of the room.

"The longer you wail, the longer you stay in there."

And then she closed the doors of the big closet and stormed out of the room, slamming the door behind her.

I got dressed and shuffled over to the table. It was impossible to eat. Bernardo, Mary and I stared at the Cream of Wheat in our bowls. It was cold and jellied, and we stirred it glumly, listening to Cindy's crying go on and on.

And then someone opened the door to our ward. The sunlight shone behind her and I could have sworn it was Glinda, the Good Witch of the East, arriving in her magical glitter.

It was Tante Marie.

She saw me and swept over to the table, bringing the light with her, surrounding the three of us where we sat, amazed, with the fresh scent of lavender.

"Oh, Paulie. *C'est toi, chérie?* Is it you?" She knelt beside me and wrapped her arms around me.

"I came as soon as I could. It's so good to see you."

I was dazzled. Overwhelmed. I didn't speak. But I sure held on tight. I rubbed my nose against her soft cheek, breathing in the sweet smell of her. Tante Marie ... *here*.

"There's an awful nurse down the hall," she said. "Dreadful woman. Don't tell me she's yours? She didn't want to let me in. She told me I'd have to wait until Sunday, like the other visitors. Can you believe that? After coming all the way from Paris to see you?"

"Mother Mary and the Holy Ghost," B stammered, staring at her with enormous eyes. "That must be Witch Wilson. She's our nurse all right. She's the head nurse. You're going to get thrown out – even if you are an angel."

"Witch Wilson?" Tante Marie repeated thoughtfully. "I have no intention of being thrown out by Witch Wilson."

She stared at our breakfast. The cereal looked like white cement. Witch Wilson never gave us milk or sugar – she said we'd just spill it if she put it on the table for us.

Then Tante Marie heard the whimpering. She stood up.

"What's that I hear? Someone crying?"

I nodded. So did Bernardo and Mary. But none of us were speaking.

She scrunched her eyebrows, perplexed. She began

to walk around the room, going from crib to crib. She smiled warmly at Frank, Stan and Philip on the boys' side, then Lorna on the girls' side. There were two empty cribs where Mary and I slept, and a big empty space between them where Cindy's crib should have been.

Tante Marie stared at the empty space. Then she walked in the direction of the crying.

She stood in front of the closed closet. I thought my heart was going to jump right out of my chest. Would she dare open it? Someone should warn her. She wasn't allowed to do that. Witch Wilson would …

Tante Marie flung the closet door open wide. I could only see her back, which seemed to stiffen with horror for a moment. And then she went inside, close to Cindy. She knelt over and put her head near Cindy's. I could hear the calm, soft murmur of Tante Marie's voice, soothing, reassuring.

Gradually Cindy's crying turned to whimpering and then even that stopped. Tante Marie stood up again and – I couldn't believe it – she pushed Cindy's bed out of the closet.

Oh boy! There was going to be trouble!

I heard Tante Marie's voice, clear as a bell. I bet the whole hospital could. "What a strange thing, putting you in the closet. The nurse made a terrible mistake. But it won't happen again, I promise you. Never, ever again. Now let me put you right back where your bed belongs beside the other children. I'll get you cleaned up and then something good to eat."

That's just what she did. She hummed that song all my aunts and Grand-mère sang when they got together. I had no idea what it meant. It was one of those French songs they were always singing and it sounded pretty.

Cindy's face was brightening with Tante Marie beside her. She wasn't exactly happy, but she didn't look scared anymore.

Next, Tante Marie went over to Philip. Philip was the youngest, only four. He lay paralyzed in his crib opposite Cindy. He'd been here seven months already, but could only wriggle his toes.

"I'm Pauline's aunt," Tante Marie introduced herself. "You can call me Tante Marie. Now I want you to tell me what I can do for you."

"Can you find my teddy?" Philip asked in a hopeful voice.

Philip's teddy had fallen out of his crib during the night and lay on the floor.

"He's right here," Tante Marie said, picking him up, pretending she was whispering something in the teddy's ear before tucking him in tight beside Philip.

"Teddy told me he was wondering where *you* were all night."

Philip laughed.

Tante Marie went around the room, introducing herself to everyone, asking what they needed. Part of me was getting mad, having to wait so long for my turn. But then I told myself to wait. She was like Christmas, coming for everybody. And I was lucky to have her for the rest of my life. I could share her a little bit with my friends.

B gave her a daring look and asked her if she could get some milk and sugar for our cereal.

"I'd be happy to," she said.

She must have seen the look of longing in my eyes. I didn't know how much longer I could wait. She knelt down beside me and whispered in my ear, "I'll be right back, *ma belle*. Then it will be you and me, don't worry."

She left the door open. We heard her heels, clicking down the hallway. Then we heard voices beginning to argue. Tante Marie's was firm and insistent.

I looked at B. He had a huge smile. "I like your Tante Marie," he said. "I'm going to marry her when I grow up."

If she ever comes back! I thought. What if they threw her out? It was taking too long. What was happening?

Before I could worry more, I heard her clicking heels again, and Tante Marie was back, carrying a sugar bowl and a pitcher of milk. She put them on the table for us and knelt once more between B and me. "*Et voilà.* I got them to heat the milk for you. It's much better hot, don't you think?"

I swear B's eyes melted. He leaned over and gave her a big, smacking kiss. "You said it, Tante Marie!"

We heard the unmistakable sound of feet stomping down the hallway. Witch Wilson's feet.

Sure enough, Witch Wilson appeared in the doorway. Her eyes blazed and she pointed an accusing finger at Tante Marie. Behind her she had the doctor in tow.

"That's her. That's the one. Barged right in here when we're trying to work. She's going to make someone sick …"

Cindy let out a piercing, hysterical scream. "No! No! Don't lock me in the closet again. Please don't put me back in there."

Quickly Tante Marie walked over and released the side of Cindy's crib. It came down with a crash. She scooped Cindy into her arms, cradling the sobbing girl with her protective warmth. "There, there. No one's ever going to lock you in the closet again, are they?"

She fired a look at Witch Wilson, a look that said everything.

The doctor was watching quietly, taking it all in.

Then B pretended to cry too. "Oh, Nurse Wilson. You won't lock me in the closet again, will you? Or take my meals away? Please, please."

"Nurse Wilson," the doctor said grimly, pointing to the hallway. "I'd like to see you in my office, *now*."

Witch Wilson left. In disbelief, I watched her turn

and leave our ward. It was like having a nightmare leave. Morning sunlight brightened the room. Yes! She was gone. In the seconds following her departure, the room gradually filled with the normal, safe sounds of our breathing – then our grumbling, hungry stomachs, all mixed with the smells of breakfast, our unwashed bodies and the dreamy scent of lavender that accompanied my Tante Marie.

B got up from the table, walked to the doorway and peered down the hallway after the doctor and Witch Wilson.

He came back into the room, shut the door and raised his hands over his head triumphantly. "Boy, is she getting it good!"

We cheered, banging our cribs or tables with cups, spoons or leg braces, whatever we could manage.

B sat down at the table again. "Am I ever hungry. Nothing like a fight to work up an appetite," he said and poured the entire bowl of sugar, then the pitcher of hot milk, over our three small bowls of cereal.

I couldn't eat. I was watching Tante Marie, waiting. She tucked Cindy comfortably back in her bed and then, finally, finally walked toward me.

My turn.

Tante Marie knelt beside me, close, and I looked into her deep brown eyes, now only a few inches from mine.

With her fingertips, she brushed my bangs out of my eyes and whispered in my ear words that were only meant for me. "*Ma belle*. My beautiful, special one, Pauline. I had to save you for last. I knew I could count on you to wait so patiently. What can I do for you, *chérie*?"

That's when my voice finally came out of hiding. It crawled up from some place deep inside me. For the first time in ten months I spoke.

"Please, Tante Marie. Can you take me home?"

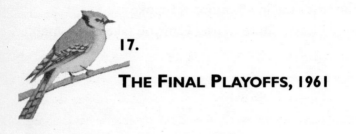

17.

THE FINAL PLAYOFFS, 1961

Tante Marie and I arrange ourselves at opposite ends of the window seat for the playoffs.

My blue Maple Leafs are ready for a face-off at center. The Canadiens get the puck and there's a shot on goal. Johnny Bower makes a brilliant save.

It dawns on me that my parents and new sister could be home any minute. The week – my private time with Tante Marie – will end as soon as they arrive. "I wish you could stay a few weeks longer," I say.

"Me too," she nods.

"It's so different when you're here. We're happier."

"We? Do you think your maman is happier too?" she laughs, mocking me gently.

"Sometimes I wonder if you two are really sisters," I say, whacking the puck down the miniature rink.

"What's she got against you?"

"What's with you tonight? So many questions!"

"No one around here talks to me. I don't understand this family. And ..." All my worry rushes to the surface, freeing itself. "I'm about to be a sister. What if we fight like you and my mother?"

Tante Marie looks sad. "Oh, Pauline. I hope not. What do you want to know? You want to understand your maman?"

I nod.

"The first thing to understand about her is that she always loved books. Just like you with your hockey. Grand-mère used to say Agathe was born with a book in her hand. And I remember, when I was eight, she won a scholarship to study English literature here in Toronto. You'd think she'd won a million dollars. It meant the world to her."

"Why isn't she teaching at the university anymore if she loves it so much?"

A pained look comes over Tante Marie. I've never seen her hesitate like this.

"The summer you became sick with polio," she says slowly, choosing her words, "she was about to become a professor at the *université*. She was French. She was a woman. You can't imagine how hard she'd worked to get there."

"I spoiled her life ... is that what you're trying to say?"

"No!" She shakes her head emphatically. "She loved you more than all the books in the world, and all the students. I can only imagine how she felt watching you. You were very, very sick. They nearly lost you. They were at the mercy of the iron lung and the doctors and the hospitals."

She shudders, remembering. I do too.

"It was such a miracle that you got better and walked again. Surely you can understand that after all that helpless, anxious waiting, there was nothing more important than that?"

I don't say anything.

"Right or wrong, Agathe gave up her life at the *université* because you'd had too much hurt. And in the beginning, it made sense. You needed exercising and home-schooling. She wanted to protect you."

My mother gave up her life for me. She sacrificed herself. If only she hadn't. How different these last years would have been if she'd let me go to school. But still, something doesn't make sense. "Why didn't she protect me in the hospitals?"

Tante Marie groans. "Oh. Those hospitals." She hugs me for a long minute. She wipes a tear from her eye. "How did you survive them, *chérie*? You and your friends." She lets out a deep breath. "You can't blame your maman. The hospital was taking care of you and your parents had to trust them. You were all at their mercy. Every week you got stronger. And remember . . ."

She pauses. "You didn't speak. They came every visiting day. You seemed to be getting better and you didn't tell them what was going on."

"But why was it you … you!"

She throws her hand up as if to God. "Oh, Pauline! You sound like Agathe. Just thank God it was someone! I happened to come that morning. I'd been so far away and felt so desperate to see you. I happened to see what the horrible woman was doing. You know what's crazy? I was the best person, and the worst person, to save you. At first your maman was grateful. But later, she turned it against me. As if I'd done it on purpose. She wished it had been *her* to save you. I stole that from her."

She shakes her head and looks sadly out the window. "It's strange how things happen in life. Grand-mère once told me that Agathe resented me the moment I was born."

She squeezes my hand. "Grand-mère. She was such a wise woman. I miss talking to her. I used to ask her, why do people get the problems they do? Why did Pauline get polio? Why did I get Agathe for my older sister? You know what Grand-mère used to say?"

I shake my head, remembering Grand-mère as I saw her on Christmas Eve, with a crown of red velvet ribbons against her white hair. "She said that we get what we can handle. It's like hanging our wash out on the laundry line in the backyard. If we all looked outside and saw each other's problems hanging out on their lines, we would each choose our own line, and reel it back in."

Out the window, I see that the pools of water on my backyard rink are shrinking as they freeze. I wonder suddenly what Henry's problems would look like on a laundry line, or Stuart's or Billy's. Or my mother's.

"Hey! Let's finish our match before they get home," Tante Marie says.

We throw ourselves into the game. It's a tied game, and in the last minute, Tante Marie knocks over one of my forwards and I make a buzzing sound. "Penalty!" I holler.

For the last minute, I tell her, she has to play sitting on one hand. Somehow she manages to score immediately from the face-off, and this seems hilarious to both of us.

"With one hand! I beat Toronto with one hand!" she hoots.

She scoops me up and swings me around, my left leg flapping wildly.

"*Maudits anglais!* Those damn Englishmen!" we laugh and scream.

We don't hear my parents come in.

"*Arrêt, Marie!* That's enough." The brittle voice of my mother stops us.

My parents stand in the doorway, watching. My

mother's holding a small bundle that must be a baby. Her face is drawn and upset. A chill has entered the room with her – a glacier is moving over us. My feet slide awkwardly to the floor and I stand, holding onto Tante Marie. If only we'd heard them come in.

"What are you doing now, Marie? Trying to turn her against the English? Do you forget this is Toronto, our home?"

"Agatha. They're playing, having fun," my father pleads.

Everything about my mother seems to be cracking: her face, her hands. Afraid, I watch her thrust the small bundle – my sister – toward my father. In a shattered voice, my mother says, "You always take Marie's side, Will. But I know she wants to divide us, to cause trouble. I want her to leave."

She turns abruptly and runs up the stairs. We hear the click of her door.

A strange feeling comes over me, as if I'm looking in one of those curved mirrors at a circus. We are turning into skinny giants, fat midgets, an unrecognizable family.

My dad breaks the awkward silence. His voice comes from far away and he sounds tired. "You'll have to forgive her. It's been a long week and she's not herself. She was up all last night with the baby and she's exhausted. We should all get to bed. Things will look better in the morning."

The baby fusses. She sounds strange, like a little cat meowing. Tante Marie gives me my crutches and goes to stand beside my father. She pulls back the blanket gently.

"You have another beautiful daughter. Let me hold her, Will. Just for a minute. I won't get a chance tomorrow in front of Agathe."

Tante Marie sways from side to side, admiring what's in the bundle.

"Did you pick a name yet?"

"Céline," he answers.

"A good French name," she says approvingly. She rubs her cheek gently against the baby's, whispering *Céline*, then gives her back to my dad.

"Things will never change between us," Marie says quietly. Dad shakes his head, starting to protest.

"You know I'm right, Will. I'll leave early in the morning. She'll find it too hard to have me here. You'll take me to the train station and I'll get the first train back to Montréal. Having a new baby is a big adjustment. It will be easier for everybody with me gone."

Not for me, I want to say. Only for my mother.

Dad sighs like he's too tired to argue, and switches off the light.

"*Bonne nuit*," Tante Marie says, in the dark. "You look tired too. Go up to bed and I'll say goodnight to Pauline."

"I know Agatha appreciates your coming, even if

she can't say it. Thank you, Marie," he says. He looks over at me. "Sleep well, Pauline. Goodnight." And before I can stop him, he too disappears up the stairs.

The house is so suddenly quiet, I hear the furnace click on in the basement and the air come *whooshing* up the vents. For a second, I feel like I'm back in the iron lung and it is pressing, pressing on me, forcing me to breathe.

Adults are so complicated. I wish I could cry like a baby.

But then I look at Tante Marie's face. In the moonlight, years of hurt are reflected in her eyes, though she tries to blink it away, and I want only one thing: to cheer her up.

"I'm a big sister," I say. "How long before I can teach that kid to play goal?"

Tante Marie laughs and wipes her eyes. "Knowing you, next year. As soon as Céline can walk."

She walks over to me and kisses both my cheeks – the smell of Tante Marie. "I'll be gone in the morning," she continues. "I won't come back here again."

My legs tremble at the thought of losing her. It's not fair. "But if you don't come, I'll never see you."

"The train runs both ways between Toronto and Montréal," Tante Marie says.

"Me?" It's an astonishing thought. Could I do it? "Travel alone on the train?"

"You'll be fourteen in August. I traveled alone

when I was twelve. There's a porter to help you on and off. And the conductor will treat you like a queen. You'll love it."

Tante Marie's eyes sparkle. "If I send you the ticket for your birthday, your maman won't deny you my gift."

The pressing on my chest stops. I realize it wasn't pressure on my lungs at all. It was on my heart. My mother's problems are not mine. I can still love Tante Marie.

"I'll do it. I'll come by myself."

She drops her voice to a whisper, a lavender-scented whisper. "We'll have fun. I'll take you to see *les Canadiens* play at the Forum. That's where we'll really beat those *maudits anglais.*"

Oh, Tante Marie! She makes me laugh. How lucky I am. Ever since that first time back in the House of Horrors, she's brought me her gifts. She causes such wonderful trouble.

If only my mother could understand. Whatever Tante Marie's gifts, they have a way of bringing me home.

18.

HOME

In the morning when I get up, Tante Marie is gone. Dad has taken her to the train station. She is on her way back to Montréal. She's on her way home.

As I get dressed, I remember the trouble she caused at the House of Horrors. We had to wait a few days until I could be discharged. Tante Marie visited every morning, staying for hours to check that we were all okay. She brought fresh croissants, raspberry jam and thermoses of hot chocolate, teaching us to sing "*Alouette, gentille Alouette*" with her as we got ready for each day.

Witch Wilson quit, or was fired. It didn't matter which. When the doctor ordered her down to his office, she left our ward for the last time. She never haunted us again.

My mother is right about Tante Marie. She has always caused trouble. Wonderful trouble.

I understand now that my mother blamed herself when I finally spoke and told them about all the bad things I'd had to endure. I guess that's why she was so afraid to let me go to school. She was afraid I'd get mistreated or hurt again.

I know what it's like to be jealous and hate somebody for what they can do, especially when it's something you find hard or can't do very well yourself. I think my mother feels that way about her youngest sister, Marie.

I love Tante Marie. But I also love my mother.

I walk into the kitchen. My mother is holding my sister, my new sister Céline. I can tell by my mother's red, blotchy face that she's been crying.

Céline's got a red, blotchy face too. Oh no! Both of them.

"Hi, Mom," I say, sitting beside her. It's probably best not to bring up Tante Marie and what happened last night. Besides – this itsy-bitsy sister is amazing!

"Oh, Mom. She's so tiny. Look at her fingers. Just like a doll. I can't believe it."

My mother looks up at me. Her hair is a thick brown mess, hanging loosely to her shoulders. She looks like she hasn't had much sleep.

"Would you like to hold her?"

I reach out my arms. Mom cradles her, carefully

passing her into my arms.

"She hardly weighs a thing! She feels like a warm football."

My mother laughs. "Oh, Pauline."

Oh no. Now she looks like she's going to cry again.

"You'll be such a better sister than I ever was."

Well. What should I say to that? I suppose she knows she doesn't treat Tante Marie fairly. But I know better than to rub it in. So I say nothing.

"I … I reacted badly last night. I'm sorry," she says.

What has happened to my mother?

She pushes her hair off her face, finds a comb in her pocket and begins to tidy her hair as she speaks. "I wondered if you might like to see Tante Marie this summer for your birthday."

I'm not sure I've heard her right. She keeps combing her hair, arranging herself, pulling herself together.

She puts the comb back in her pocket and looks at me uncertainly. "You'll be old enough to go on your own this summer. Maybe you could take the train to Montréal … it might be an adventure."

It's on the tip of my tongue to tell her that I've already planned it with Tante Marie.

And then I realize something – Mom's trying. She's trying to let me be independent. She's trying to give me a gift.

"Do you think I could? All by myself?" I ask, trying to sound a little fearful.

"I do. You are full of surprises, Pauline. You are a very capable person," she says.

Slowly, carefully, I pass her back my little sister. "You're full of surprises yourself, Mom."

We laugh together, looking at the baby. We both know I mean *more* than the baby.

She seems proud. "Not bad for an old grouch of forty."

"Nearly forty-one!" I remind her.

There's a knock at the side door.

"I bet that's Henry," I say. "They want to play on the rink. Okay, Mom?" I hold my breath, unsure of her answer. Dad's not home yet. He's still at Union Station with Tante Marie. Mom doesn't like me on the ice with anyone but Dad.

My sister helps out – she starts to cry. Mom rocks her, looking from me to Céline, somewhat anxious. "I'm not sure. Céline's hungry and I should feed her. Those boys might push you too fast."

"They're careful, Mom. Don't worry." I get up as quickly as I can to answer the door, before she can change her mind.

"Hey, Henry. Are the other guys here?"

"Yup. Need any help?"

I've been letting my hair grow long. It swings around my shoulders as I lean forward to give him my crutches. I take my red beret and coat off the hook on the wall and get ready. I am aware of Henry watching me, holding the side door for me.

"What did you do to your hair?" he asks.

"What's wrong with it?"

He's looking at me funny. I take my crutches from him and smile as I walk past him.

"Nothing," he answers. "Remember when we used to ride our horses up and down the lawns and your long hair would fly behind you? You used to say you had a horse's mane."

I laugh suddenly, remembering. "And you wanted to grow your hair long too, Henry. I remember the big fight you had with your mom."

Henry hoots. "I'd forgotten that. Do you know there's a weird guy at school who's got long hair? He wears it in a ponytail. I wonder if he fights with his mother about it."

"Maybe I'll ask him that when I meet him at school."

Henry does a double-take. "You mean … you're coming to school? What about your mom?"

"I think I can persuade her. I want to take music, maybe play the drums or the trumpet in the school band."

"What about the stairs?"

"I'll do them," I say firmly. "It'll be good exercise. Anyway, so what if I'm a few minutes late to a few classes. I'm a few years late! A few minutes is nothing."

Henry laughs. "You know, I've been thinking.

There's a little freight elevator the caretaker uses for supplies and moving desks and stuff."

I stare at him, amazed. He's been thinking about me.

"The caretaker's name is Mr. Shine. Honest. He's just like his name. He'd give you a ride —"

I interrupt him, feeling a little annoyed. "I'm not freight, Henry. I'll do the stairs."

"Okay, Pauline. It was just a suggestion."

He looks a little hurt. My mind jumps back to another scene, another time when he was thinking about me. "Do you remember that day you brought me the sheriff's badge, Henry?"

He looks a bit puzzled, but nods.

"I couldn't move my fingers or hands until that day. You put the badge on the window and I was so happy, I wanted it so badly, I moved my fingers for the first time."

Henry has a strange look on his face. "I didn't realize that. I always thought ... you know ... I misunderstood. I thought you were telling me to go away."

"Yeah. Well. You've got hair on your face." I have no idea why I say it. It comes out of nowhere. It's just, all of a sudden, I don't know what else to say and I notice a fuzz of hair on Henry's cheeks. There'll be other times to talk about what happened in the past. This is too important, though. How could I not have noticed the hair on Henry's face?

He rolls his eyes at me. "Geez, Pauline. You still

say the darndest things."

Stuart and Billy are bringing the wheelchair out of the garage.

"Hey, guys. Guess what? Pauline's coming to school. We just gotta work on her mom."

Billy's carrying our hockey sticks and claps them together. "Great."

Henry sits on the little bench next to the opening in the sideboards. He takes off his boots and begins to put on his skates.

Stuart has a strange look on his face.

"What's wrong, Stu?" I ask.

"I don't know. I just can't figure why you guys think school's such a good idea for Pauline."

They've been talking about this amongst themselves. All of them.

Stuart continues, "I'd rather stay home all day and watch TV."

I turn myself around to sit in the wheelchair. Henry is busy, lacing up his skates. Billy does just what my dad would do, if he were here. He stands behind the wheelchair to secure it as I sit down. I drop my crutches to the ground.

Henry's voice is low and impatient. "Stu, you'd do better at school if you thought about things a little more. Imagine watching TV all day. Come on. Remember summer holidays? How sick you get of it after two days? It's boring staying at home. Pauline'll have a way better time with all of us at school than home alone."

He stands up and passes me the goalie stick.

Stuart grumbles. "I still think we should ask Pauline's mom if we can all home-school with her."

"She'd make you read Charles Dickens and Jane Austen."

"Who are they?"

"You wouldn't like them," Henry says. "Let's play two-on-two."

"I don't want to play goalie today," I say, staring at Henry. "I know my dad's not here, but we don't need him. It's my turn to be forward."

Darn, my voice sounds squeaky, like a mouse. The three boys tower over me, their faces worried. For a second, I lose my nerve.

I pull my red beret a little lower over my forehead. Dangerous. "I've got a great shot. Who wants to be on my team?"

Billy offers me his stick. "Me. You be my forward. We'll play open goal."

Henry walks over quickly on the tips of his skates and stands behind my chair. He has that look on his face when he's determined to have things his way. Firm mouth, eyes blazing. He edges Billy out of the way.

"No way. Pauline's mine. I'll push her. And we get to come back to play goal too."

"How are you going to get back fast enough?" Stu

asks. "How's that going to work?"

Henry laughs. "You've got no imagination, Stuie. Just play. You'll see how fast Pauline and I are."

Billy and Stuart wait and let us go on the rink first. Henry tilts the chair back to get my feet up over the edge of the rink. The ice is winking in the sun.

Then Henry tilts me further, way back. My hair swings into the snow beneath me. I laugh, surprised. When I look up, I see Henry's face upside-down above mine and my heart beats a little faster. *Mon cœur qui bat.*

"Ready, Paulie?"

I give him a thumbs-up. "Let's fly."

Anne Laurel Carter is a hockey fan who had a hockey rink in her own childhood Don Mills backyard. She remembers her parents' stories about the polio "Summer Plague" of 1953. While this is Anne Carter's first novel for Orca, she is the author of the young adult title *The Girl on Evangeline Beach* and of the picture book *Tall in the Saddle* (Orca, 1999), a Canadian Children's Book Centre "Our Choice" selection. She is a full-time writer who still has a hockey rink in her Toronto backyard each winter.

More juvenile fiction from Orca.

THE GRAMMA WAR
Kristin Butcher

Nick and Kia, the two best basketball players in their grade, are eager to join up for the school's "Three on Three" tournament. But they'll have to play against the older grades as well. So there's only one thing to do if they are going to have any chance to win — find an older kid to join their team. Marcus, who is two grades above them and the best player in the school, is the perfect choice.

Of course, Nick and Kia have to convince Marcus to join them. And the two friends also have to avoid becoming targets for the older kids who also want Marcus on their team. This tournament is going to be a lot more tricky than they thought.

1-55143-183-1
$8.95 CAN; $6.95 USA

More juvenile fiction from Orca.

WAITING TO DIVE
Karen Rivers

Carly is ten and loves to dive — dive from the rocks at her family's summer cabin, dive from the boards at the pool with her diving-club teammates. She loves the feeling of floating up into the air and then dropping cleanly into the water with hardly a splash. She loves the feeling she gets when everything goes just right.

Then one summer weekend, as she and her friends Montana and Samantha play in the water at the cabin, things don't go just right and her world is turned upside-down.

Waiting to Dive is Karen Rivers' second novel for young readers. Her teen novel *Dream Water* (Orca, 1999) was a finalist for the Sheila Egoff Book Award. Karen lives in Victoria, BC.

1-55143-159-9
$8.95 CAN; $6.95 USA

More juvenile fiction from Orca.

PIPER
Natale Ghent

When eleven-year-old Wesley's father dies, she and her mother must move in with Aunt Cindy on a working farm. Watching the birth of a litter of Australian shepherd puppies, Wesley pleads with her aunt to save the life of a runt. The puppy, an undersized red merle named Piper, is a challenge from the start, with a natural talent for trouble as well as for herding sheep.

Through hard work and long hours, the dog and girl become inseparable and even stand a chance at the herding championship. But when Piper and Wesley are set upon by marauding coyotes, it is Piper who must protect Wesley. Will the dog save the girl who gave her a second chance? Will they still have a shot at the big title?

Piper tells the timeless story of a girl and her dog and the ties that bind them together. Natale Ghent has crafted a tale that speaks to anyone who has struggled for something they truly believe in, and for a place to call home.

1-55143-167-X
$8.95 CAN; $6.95 USA